in a perfect world

ALSO BY TRISH DOLLER

Something Like Normal

Where the Stars Still Shine

The Devil You Know

in a perfect world

TRISH DOLLER

SIMON PULSE

New York London Toronto Sydney New Delhi

SIMON PULSE

An imprint of Simon & Schuster Children's Publishing Division

1230 Avenue of the Americas, New York, New York 10020

First Simon Pulse hardcover edition May 2017

Text copyright © 2017 by Trish Doller

Jacket illustration copyright © 2017 by Sarah Dennis

All rights reserved, including the right of reproduction in whole or in part in any form.

SIMON PULSE and colophon are registered trademarks of Simon & Schuster, Inc.

For information about special discounts for bulk purchases, please contact Simon & Schuster Special Sales at 1-866-506-1949 or business@simonandschuster.com.

The Simon & Schuster Speakers Bureau can bring authors to your live event. For more information or to book an event contact the Simon & Schuster Speakers Bureau at 1-866-248-3049 or visit our website at www.simonspeakers.com.

Jacket designed by Karina Granda and Greg Stadnyk

Interior designed by Greg Stadnyk

The text of this book was set in Adobe Caslon Pro.

Manufactured in the United States of America

2 4 6 8 10 9 7 5 3 1

This book has been cataloged with the Library of Congress.

ISBN 978-1-4814-7988-2 (hc)

ISBN 978-1-4814-7990-5 (eBook)

Wherever you go, go with all your heart.

—Confucius

CHAPTER 1

My forehead is pressed to the small oval window when the Pyramids of Giza come into view. From so far overhead they remind me of the elementary school diorama I built from a shoe box and pictures cut from Grandma Irene's *National Geographic* magazines. She kept the issues stacked in neat piles on a shelf in her closet and I remember how the older ones—from the sixties and seventies—listed the topics down the yellow spine: EGYPT OTTERS ALASKA'S GLACIERS BALLOONS. I'd found three issues with articles about Egypt, and even though the magazines were in pristine condition, Grandma didn't mind me ruining the pages.

In all those photos, the pyramids seemed to stand in the middle of a vast golden sea of sand, but from this elevation, the outskirts of Cairo bump up against them in a way I would have never expected. Through the hazy layer of smog that hangs over the city, everything is the same color as the desert—if there are trees down there, I can't see them yet—and the Nile meanders through the middle like a dark ribbon.

"That island right there is where we'll be living." Mom touches her fingertip to the window as the plane begins its descent, but there are a few islands in the river and it doesn't really matter which one she's talking about. Instead I seek out soccer fields, backyard swimming pools, housing developments, thick green clumps of parks—anything that might make Cairo resemble Cleveland or Chicago or New York City. Might make Egypt seem less . . . foreign. Except when the flight attendant reminds us to fasten our seat belts for landing, she does it first in Arabic, then in English, reminding me that this city—our new home—is six thousand miles from the one we left behind.

Our new home.

I press a nervous palm against the metal buckle of the belt that's been strapped across my lap for the better part of two days. Since we left Frankfurt nearly four hours ago. Since the eight-hour flight across the Atlantic from Newark. Since the two-hour hop from Cleveland.

This isn't the first time I've flown—we take yearly trips to visit Uncle Mike and his family in the Florida Keys—but this journey has worn me down. I know I should be excited about landing in a *completely different country* for the first time ever, but there is a toddler in 18B who won't stop crying. The man sitting behind me keeps thumping the back of my seat every time he moves his legs.

And I can't stop thinking about everything I've given up.

My summer plans were locked down. Hannah and I had been hired to work at one of the admissions gates at Cedar Point. Owen came up with a bucket list of things to do before graduation, like sneaking into the abandoned Prehistoric Forest at night to see the fake dinosaurs in the dark, tracking down the cemetery in Cleveland where an angel statue is said to weep, and going to the Renaissance fair dressed in costume. Also, my parents had already paid the deposit for soccer camp at Ohio State. For as long as I've been playing, my personal goal has been to make captain of the girls' team in my senior year, but now there's no chance of that happening. My not doing these things won't stop the world from spinning, but that doesn't mean I won't miss them.

"I hate this part." Mom grips both Dad's hand and mine as the plane makes its final approach. It takes a certain level of fearlessness to relocate to a country where the government is not super-stable and the fear of terrorism is real, so it's hard to believe my mother is afraid of flying. Still, I give her hand a gentle squeeze and watch out the window as the ground rushes up beneath us. The runway is in the desert, where all the colors have faded to a singular dusty tan that stretches out to the horizon, and it feels as if our destination is nowhere at all.

The wheels bump, the brakes roar, and when it is clear we've landed without crashing, Mom releases her death grip. Her mouth spreads into an excited smile and her voice lifts a couple of octaves. "We're here!"

A couple of weeks ago, Dad and I took the ferry to Kelleys Island to celebrate the end of school, a tradition he started when I was in kindergarten. Each year we spend one whole day circumnavigating the island on our bicycles, eating fried perch sandwiches at the Village Pump, and collecting stones from the state park beach on the north side. When I was little, I would gather as many stones as the basket on my bike could hold, so many that it made pedaling hard. Dad would suggest I lighten the load and made me live with the consequences when I refused. As I got older, he taught me how to wet the stones in the lake to bring out their true colors. It's still hard not to overload my basket, but I've become more discerning with age. This year my haul was just one perfect stone flecked with pink and black quartz.

On the way back to the ferry landing at Marblehead, as we stood at the rail watching a couple of kids fling bread in the air for the gulls, Dad broke the news. "You know how your mom has always wanted to work for OneVision?"

OneVision is a nongovernment global health organization like Doctors Without Borders, except OneVision provides eye examinations and glasses to people in need, and eye surgeries to restore sight. For as long as I can remember, it has been Mom's dream to work for OneVision, to help people see.

The wind whipped at my hair and I peeled a strand away from my mouth. "She said she would wait until I finish high school."

"That was always the plan, but they need her now," Dad said. "She's been asked to establish a clinic in Cairo and she really wants to say yes."

What about me?

I didn't ask the question out loud because that would have made me sound like a spoiled brat. Even thinking it felt selfish. Soccer camp and high school bucket lists were much smaller dreams than OneVision, but that didn't mean I didn't still want them.

"What about you?" I asked instead.

Dad is the captain of an offshore tugboat that pushes a gas barge up and down the East Coast. He works on an alternating schedule—two weeks on, two weeks off—which hasn't always been an easy way to live. Mom and I fall into a routine that gets disrupted whenever he comes home, and if anything important happens when he is away, Dad is not there for it. He's spent more than one Christmas at sea. He's missed soccer games, gymnastics competitions, and birthday parties. It's an unconventional way to be a family, but we manage.

"I have to keep my job," he said.

"Can't I just stay with you?"

"How would that work?"

"I'm seventeen," I pointed out, but he gave me a look that even his Ray-Bans couldn't hide. One that said there was no way my parents would even consider letting me stay home alone while Dad was at sea. "Okay, so maybe I could live with Grandma and Grandpa when you're gone. Or Grandma Irene."

His eyebrows lifted above the top of his sunglasses. "You're telling me you would rather move to a retirement community filled with elder humans than to the cradle of civilization?"

"When you put it that way . . ."

"I know this is not how you imagined your senior year." Dad dragged a hand up through his salt-and-pepper hair and I caught sight of my name inked in black around his wrist like a permanent bracelet. He'd gotten the tattoo when I was one day old, just after they filled out my birth certificate. "I get it. I really do. Flights to Cairo are going to eat my time and money, but I'm willing to make the sacrifice because it is important to your mom."

"Are we going to sell the house?"

"The program requires a one-year commitment," Dad said. "So we'll rent out the house until we get back."

The thought of someone else sleeping in my bed made me ache, starting in my heart and radiating out into the rest of my body. I blinked a few times, trying not to cry, but when my dad wrapped his arms around me, I came undone.

We've lived in the same pumpkin-orange bungalow on Finch Street for as long as I've been alive. As the ferry churned through the deep, shimmering blue of Lake Erie, I could not imagine living in another house in another city in another country. Even now, as our plane taxies down the runway toward the terminal in Cairo, I still can't fully wrap my mind around it.

Dad stands in the aisle, pulling down our carry-on bags from the overhead compartment, and I inhale deeply, pushing against the tide of tears threatening to spill. There is no point in crying.

We are here.

CHAPTER 2

Aboard the plane we were travelers, in the customs line we were foreigners, but once we are beyond the concourse with our stamped passports in hand, we become strangers in Egypt. Strange ones at that. There is my punk rock dad with his tugboat tan (arms, face, not much else) and a black T-shirt that leaves his tattoo sleeves exposed for anyone to see the pin-up girl wearing an old-fashioned bathing suit and the dancing skeleton holding a martini glass. Dad is sturdy, strong, and kind of intimidating.

My mom is imposing in her own way: a million miles tall with Nordic-blond hair. She's dressed in a loose-fitting white tunic and black pants in an effort to blend in, but she looks like a Viking goddess and announces herself without saying a word. There's no way she's ever going to blend in.

Then there is me, halfway between them, with her pale hair and his pale Irish freckles. The less-cool Anna to Mom's ice queen Elsa, just trying not to be noticed at all. But as the escalator carries us down to the baggage claim, people are staring. At her. At me. Particularly the men, who drag their gazes from my hair to my chest—even though my red bandanna-print top covers me completely—then look quickly away when Dad glares.

"Christ," he mutters under his breath. "This is going to be a long year."

At the bottom of the escalator, amid taxi drivers and chauffeurs, stands a man about my parents' age with a neatly clipped goatee, black-rimmed glasses, and graying hair. He holds a sign that has KELLY FAMILY printed on it in bold black letters.

"We are the Kelly family," my dad says.

"Welcome to Egypt." The man's smile is wide as he speaks with a heavy accent. "I am your driver, Ahmed Saleh Elhadad."

"*Shokran.*"

My mother, the overachiever, spent the entire trip plugged into a computer program to learn the Egyptian dialect for her work in the clinic, but hearing my dad thank the driver in Arabic catches me by surprise. As Mom practices her Arabic on Mr. Elhadad, I raise my eyebrows at Dad.

He shrugs. "I figured it can't hurt to know a few words.

'Please' and 'thank you' go a long way just about everywhere."

On his very first tugboat job as a deckhand—when he was only a little older than I am now—my dad flew to Panama to meet his boat, passed through the Panama Canal, and ended up in Peru. He's worked in Mexico, Cuba, and Honduras, up and down both coasts of the United States, and in several other South American countries, so he knows a thing or two about living in the world, outside of Ohio.

The four of us walk to the baggage carousel and it is hard not to stare back at the people around me, especially the women. I am surprised to see some of them with their hair flowing around their shoulders or knotted in buns. I thought wearing a hijab was part of the rules. At least that's what Grandma Irene's favorite TV news channel would have people believe about Islam—that women are forced by a cruel religion to cover themselves.

There *are* girls wearing hijabs, but the girl walking past me dressed in skinny jeans and strappy sandals—a stack of multicolored bangle bracelets climbing up the long sleeve of her shirt—kind of makes me wish I'd pushed a little harder when Mom and I argued over what I couldn't bring to Egypt. Many—but not all—of the older women are cloaked in black abayas and hijabs, while a few wear veils over the lower part of their faces. These women unsettle me because their identities, their personalities, are concealed. Are they happy? Sad?

With their mouths covered, it feels as if they've been silenced. I glance back at the girl with the skinny jeans as she stands beside her carry-on. Clearly the rules are more complex than I thought. But if Muslim women have a choice in what they wear, why would they choose to cover themselves up?

I look away, focusing on the conveyor belt as I wait for my suitcase to come around. Fragments of conversations flow around me and Arabic seems like a harsh and unyielding language that I will never be able to understand. Overwhelmed, I limit my world—at least for now—to the search for one big lime-green duffel bag.

"Caroline, Mr. Elhadad will be the person you call when you want to go somewhere outside our immediate neighborhood," Mom says.

She overloaded me with so many rules of etiquette that I can't remember if I am supposed to shake hands with him. If so, which hand? I smile, nod in his direction, and say hello in English.

To my relief, he does the same. "My home is not so far from Manial. I will take you wherever you would like to visit. Perhaps the pyramids or to the mall."

"*Shokran.*" I test out the word for myself, even though I can't really see myself asking him to drive me anywhere. Dad is staying only long enough to see us settled, and Mom has to start almost immediately at the clinic. Where would I go by myself? Until classes begin at the American school in September, I'll probably get a jump on my required summer reading (for once), watch movies on Netflix, and video chat with Hannah. I doubt I'll have much need of Mr. Elhadad's services.

Bags in hand, we follow the driver toward the exit, and as the doors slide back, we are assaulted by a heat that feels like standing in front of an open oven. Dry. Brutal. Mom insisted the two of us dress modestly out of respect for the culture, so my duffel is filled with tunic-length tops, loose-fitting jeans, maxi dresses, and cardigans for when I am out in public. I have no idea how I will survive the summer without shorts and tank tops—my Ohio summer wardrobe—when it's so hot I can barely breathe.

Mr. Elhadad's black sedan has a few small dings and a license plate that looks more like art than information, and we practically dive into the car to get out of the heat. Dad sits in the passenger seat, but as the car merges into the thick Cairo traffic, I'm not convinced there's any advantage to riding shotgun. There seem to be no rules of the road. Cars stop abruptly in the middle of the street to let out passengers. Other cars weave in and out of traffic without warning, coming frighteningly close to my window. Pedestrians cross whenever and wherever they can. We pass a motorbike loaded with three guys, one of whom blows a kiss at me. Also, the honking is constant.

We stop and start, speed and slow, making our way down a corridor lined with apartment towers made of both ornate stone and bland concrete, their ground floors occupied by businesses, some of which I can't identify because their names are spelled out in Arabic. Past ancient mosques and modern office blocks. Past older women laden with shopping bags and men walking arm in arm down the edges of the road. Past street corners piled with garbage bags. Cairo feels like a time-lapse video compared to my sleepy little hometown.

Finally we cross a bridge over a slender canal of the Nile onto Rhoda Island and all of us—even our driver—exhale and the world seems to slow down. Before we reach the next bridge, one that would carry us across the wider part of the river into Giza, Mr. Elhadad curves onto a road running along the western edge of the island. To the left are waterfront parks filled with leafy trees and slender palms, and piers where tour boats are docked. Mr. Elhadad comes to a double-parked halt in front of a yellow nine-story curved apartment building right across the street from the Nile.

My dad whistles low. "Pretty fancy view."

"This is a very good area," Mr. Elhadad says. "Safe. Many restaurants, shops, and cinemas. I am a big fan of American film. Steve McQueen."

"Hell yeah!" Dad winces when he realizes he used profanity—

Mom explained that swearing is not something Muslims usually do—but the driver only laughs and gives my dad a thumbs-up.

Mr. Elhadad unloads our luggage from the trunk of his car and accepts a tip of several colorful Egyptian bills from my dad's wallet. The driver offers to help carry our suitcases up to the apartment, but Mom is already heading toward the front of the building, her bag rolling along behind her.

"I think we've got this," Dad says. "But thank you."

The vestibule is open and deep, with a bank of mailboxes and an elevator. Here we encounter another person who wants to help us carry our luggage. This time he's a turbaned older man whose skinny dark legs stick out from the bottom of his galabia. He taps his chest and says, "Masoud. *Bowab*."

"Masoud is the doorman," Mom says as the man presses the button to call down the elevator. "As I understand it, the *bowab* is kind of a jack-of-all-trades paid by the residents of the building to act as a security guard, gather the mail, carry packages, and even fetch groceries."

Masoud says something in Arabic and reaches for Mom's bag, but she waves him off. As we step into the elevator, carrying our own suitcases, he sags with disappointment.

The elevator stops on the third floor and Mom does the honors of unlocking the front door, which swings in to reveal a huge, sunny apartment with both French and louvered doors that open onto a long balcony overlooking the river. There are two living spaces, a dining room, and two bedrooms, all painted pristine white and still smelling of fresh paint. My room is the last room of the apartment, on the curve, with its own set of doors onto the balcony. It's enormous compared to my bedroom back home and excitement flutters inside me like paper in a breeze. I couldn't bring many keepsakes—a few photos, my favorite books, and the pink Kelleys Island stone—so my Cairo bedroom is a blank slate.

The whole apartment is beautiful, but as the tap of our heels on the wood floor echoes through the empty rooms, Mom's eyebrows draw closer and closer together. Whatever is bothering her is cut short when the call to prayer begins from a nearby mosque. The melody is as eerie as it is beautiful, but unsettling in the same way as the veiled women at the airport. Fear of the unknown. I don't understand what is being sung— or why. A few seconds later, another call from another mosque begins, overlapping with the first like a song in rounds. The second call is different, slower and mournful. We step out onto the balcony to listen, and from a more distant somewhere, a third call drifts on the air.

"So we're going to hear this five times a day, huh?" Dad slides his arm around Mom's waist.

She nods. "The morning call happens before sunrise."

"We probably should have considered that when we rented a place a block from a mosque."

"Cairo is the city of a thousand minarets," Mom says. "There are mosques *everywhere*. This is just something we're going to have to get used to."

"Those words"—he kisses her, then grins—"are going to come back to haunt you at four in the morning."

"Hello!" A deep male voice calls out from the open doorway and a tall man with a thick black beard enters the apartment, half hidden by the potted palm he carries. "I am Mohammed Taleb, the rental agent. Welcome to Cairo."

"Thank you." Mom is polite, but her words are clipped, her tone frosty. And her eyebrows have resumed the position. This is Dr. Rebecca Kelly when she is trying not to Hulk out on someone. "Where is the furniture?"

"The furniture?" Mr. Taleb blinks and swings his head in my dad's direction, but Dad just lifts his shoulders like *can't help you, dude.*

Mom takes a file folder from her tote bag and holds up a screen capture from the real estate website that touts the apartment as furnished. "I paid the deposit for a furnished apartment."

The rental agent places the palm on the floor. "Well, you see—"

"We have just spent two days traveling from the United

States. We are very tired and we have no beds. I do not want excuses, Mr. Taleb. I want solutions."

His mouth snaps shut and again he looks to my dad for support. Mom pulls the rental agreement from the folder and clicks her pen. "If I could just get your signature here, we will adjust the price to reflect the apartment's unfurnished status."

"No, no," Mr. Taleb protests. "I have a cousin who will bring you furniture tomorrow."

"Will it be the furniture in the photos?"

"No, but—"

"Then we will provide our own." She hands him the pen. He scowls as he scrawls his name at the bottom of the contract. "Now," she says. "Which hotel will you be booking us into for the night?"

CHAPTER 3

The last place Mom and I expected to end up on our first full day in Cairo is IKEA, but after spending a lumpy-bed night in a run-down hotel that Mr. Taleb claimed was world-class—with cars honking outside our window all night long—my mother was determined not to spend a second night. There is a kind of comfort that comes with walking the familiar pathways through the IKEA displays, smelling the sawdust-meets-cinnamon-roll scent as we scoop up things we need. Especially when everything outside the store feels so alien.

Mom arranges to have the larger furniture delivered, but we overfill Mr. Elhadad's sedan with bedding, bathroom supplies, and all things kitchen for the new apartment.

"My son has the afternoon off from his job," he says, gently pushing the trunk closed. What didn't fit in the trunk is piled in the backseat, leaving just enough room for me. "I will send him to help assemble your furniture."

"We can't ask your son to give up his free time for us," Mom says.

"He is skilled with his hands," Mr. Elhadad says. "And he will be grateful for the money."

That last part takes up the extra space in the car, and I feel squished between my privilege and a giant blue IKEA bag filled with whisks and bath mats and lightbulbs. Guilty for being able to pay someone to drive us around, to assemble furniture we could assemble ourselves.

My parents have done well for themselves, but we aren't extravagant people. Grandpa Jim built washing machines in a factory until he retired. He and Grandma Rose were survivors of the Great Depression who raised my mom and her siblings to live modestly. Dad's father worked in a body shop in the Bronx until the day he died. My old yellow Honda was Mom's first car out of college and my dad spends more time under the hood than I spend behind the wheel. Our house in Ohio is not a mansion by any stretch of the imagination, but living under budget is how we can afford to be in Cairo now, packed into a car with enough home goods to fill . . . well, a home. Except none of that can erase the divide between us and our driver, or my feeling embarrassed by it.

Mr. Elhadad doesn't seem bothered as he hurtles through traffic, humming along with the jangling Arabic music playing on his car radio. He chats cheerfully with Masoud as the two men tote the bags up to the apartment. Both men are tipped and barely away when my dad comes home with a dozen plastic grocery bags dangling from his fists.

"The closest supermarket is about a three-minute walk from here," Dad says. "It's tiny by American standards, but they have a lot of the basics, just different brands and Arabic labels. I stocked up on canned goods, but maybe Caroline and I can track down a fresh produce market and a butcher before I have to leave."

Exploring the city with him would be better than doing so by myself. "I wish you could stay longer."

He kisses the top of my head. "Me too, kid."

We stock the kitchen and unpack the bags from IKEA, and soon our apartment isn't quite so empty. While we wait for the delivery truck, I sit on the floor in my bedroom with the balcony doors open. The noise from the traffic on the street below floats up and the breeze that comes in off the Nile does little more than push the heat around. Back home, I could jump in my car, pick up Hannah, and go cool off in the lake. Instead it's me vs. sweat (sweat is winning) and there's nowhere I can escape. I power on my laptop for the first time since we left Ohio. Waiting in my in-box is an e-mail from Hannah.

> *C—*
>
> *I started my first day at Cedar Point and it was not nearly as much fun as I expected, especially without you. It rained, some of the tourists were total jerks, and the guy who works with me at the admissions gate is from Romania. His English is pretty terrible, so explaining the simplest things takes forever. I miss you, so write soon and tell me all about your exciting new life in Egypt.*
>
> *Love you to the moon,*
>
> *—H*
>
> *P.S. Owen is miserable.*

Until two weeks ago, Owen was my boyfriend, but as soon as Dad and I returned from Kelleys Island, I went straight to Owen's house. He smiled when he opened the front door and I felt crushed with sadness. I would miss the way his face brightened whenever he saw me and I wanted to kiss him right there on his back steps. Instead I said, "We need to talk."

His smile faded—those words are the universal signal that

whatever comes next is not going to be good—and I regretted not kissing him first.

I'd spent the rest of the ferry ride thinking about Egypt. About how so many Americans never have the chance to leave their home state, let alone get to live in another country. About how my mom had worked for this. She deserved to go. But as Owen and I walked hand in hand to the park, I wanted to stay in Sandusky with him, with my friends, with everything that was familiar and safe. I told him about the move, about OneVision, and he stopped in the middle of the sidewalk, his smile renewed. "That is so awesome. Your mom has wanted that for a long time."

On our very first date, Owen showed up on our front porch and rang the doorbell, and Dad told him that if he was going to keep coming around our house, he needed to start using the back door. Dad also asked Owen to call him Casey, but that never happened. Owen slid so effortlessly, so thoroughly, into my life that it was no surprise he remembered that OneVision was my mom's dream.

"I think we should break up."

He laughed at first, then stopped when he saw the tears in my eyes. "Why?"

"I'm going to be gone for a year," I said. "Do you really want to spend the whole time video chatting with a girl seven times zones away when you could be dating someone else?"

"I don't want to date anyone else."

"It's easy to say that now, but—"

"Caroline, I love you."

"I love you, too."

"Then why are we talking about this?" He pulled his hand up inside his long-sleeved T-shirt and offered the floppy cuff to dry my eyes. That was the sweetness of Owen. "A year isn't all that long."

"What about after that, when we graduate and go to different colleges?"

I'm good enough at soccer that I might be able to play for a college team, but Owen could be a professional someday. He's already had college coaches looking at him, so he'll probably end up at a powerhouse school like Duke or Notre Dame, places I couldn't (and probably wouldn't) follow.

"I figured we'd worry about that when it happened," he said.

"It's happening now. We have to think about it."

We sat on the swings in the park, holding hands until the streetlights came on and the crickets started chirping. We didn't talk for a really long time, neither of us wanting to spoil the moment and neither of us really wanting to break up.

"It shouldn't make sense," Owen said finally. "But it does and it sucks."

I walked my swing up close to his and kissed him. Instead

of saying good-bye, we went to his house and watched a super-hero movie we'd already seen. Owen put his arm around me the way he always did and I shifted against his shoulder the way I always did. We kissed again when we said good night on his front porch, until my lips were chapped and my dad texted to remind me that my curfew was closing in.

"I don't think I can handle staying in touch with you," was the last thing Owen said to me. "No texts. No phone calls. No e-mails. It has to be a clean break."

But as I walked home, I wasn't sure such a thing really existed. Not after a lifetime of being friends and three years of dating. Feelings are knots; they have to be untangled.

Hannah's e-mail swirls up a pang of homesickness. For her. For Owen. For everything. But before the prickling behind my eyes can turn into actual tears, a heavy knock falls on the front door and the echo travels through the apartment to my room. The furniture has arrived.

We are knee-deep in cardboard, and the delivery men are emptying the last of the truck into the living room when a dark-haired guy somewhere around my age knocks on the open door frame. He scans the mess, probably wondering what he's gotten himself into, as Dad navigates the maze of boxes to greet him. "Are you here to help?"

The guy gives an almost imperceptible nod, his voice low and his mouth set in a serious line as he says, "Yes."

"Great. Come on in," Dad says. "What's your name, kid?"

"Adam Elhadad."

Even though his pronunciation carries an accent, his name is the same as two guys I know back home and it throws me. I guess I expected something more unusual than Adam. More Egyptian? More Arabic? Either way, Adam Elhadad stands a couple inches taller than Dad with tousled black curls and eyes a shade of light brown I've never seen before. "Beautiful" seems like the wrong word but it's the only word that fits, and as soon as the thought enters my head, guilt washes through me because *P.S. Owen is miserable.*

"I'm Casey Kelly." Dad shakes Adam's hand, then gestures toward Mom and me. "My wife, Rebecca, and our daughter, Caroline."

Adam nods and cracks the barest hint of a smile as he says hello to my mother, but when he turns toward me, his gaze drops and he mumbles a hello to the floor, making me wonder if I have food stuck in my teeth or have broken some unknown Egyptian rule of etiquette.

"The beds are most important." Dad leads him away, into the master bedroom. "If we get those assembled tonight, we'll call it a win."

Adam Elhadad is no one to me, but I can't help feeling slighted. I mean, not staring is an improvement over the men at the airport, but it seems like there should be some sort of middle ground. Maybe looking at me as if I exist.

"Don't take it personally," Mom says, reading my mind. "He was lowering his gaze out of respect for you."

"Looking at you wasn't disrespectful?"

She laughs a little. "I'm an old lady to him, Caroline, someone's mother. Hardly a temptation."

My face flames at the suggestion that a guy like Adam could be tempted by a girl like me, but I roll my eyes. Mothers are genetically programmed to think their daughters are the most beautiful creatures on earth. "I'm going to go build something."

The little man on the IKEA assembly instructions is confusing me when Adam enters my room and tears into the box containing the pieces of my bed. He doesn't acknowledge my presence, doesn't speak to me as he works, and the silence in the room grows so thick that I open the balcony doors to let some of it out. Cueing up a playlist of my favorite songs, I try to ignore him, but Adam has a way of tucking this one stray curl behind his ear that makes it virtually impossible. In my superlimited time in Egypt, I've noticed that the most popular hairstyle among guys my age seems to be buzzed short on the sides and longer on top, sometimes slicked with gel, but Adam's curls spring out from his head in every direction and I am half tempted to offer him an elastic band to hold them back.

He glances up just then, catching me watching him. Heat rushes to my cheeks as I look away, turning my attention back to the directions, forcing myself to figure them out. The bookcase is small enough to double as a nightstand, so it doesn't take long before I've finished.

Adam is attaching the footboard of the bed to one of the side supports as I slide the assembled bookcase against the wall.

"Do you, um—do you need some help?" I ask the back of his head.

"No, thank you." He doesn't look up and his tone is neither hostile nor cold. It's just . . . neutral.

"Okay. Whatever." Leaving the music to play (and not caring if he doesn't like it), I go out into the living room to help Mom attach the legs to the couch.

"With me at the clinic every day, you're going to be on your own a lot this summer," she says. "The school will have some events where you can meet other American kids, but I was also thinking maybe you could explore the bazaars and shops to find things that will make this place feel less like an IKEA showroom. Make it a challenge. Get to know the city, learn to haggle, and pick up a little bit of the language along the way."

I don't want to admit that I'm afraid to venture out into this loud, crazy city alone. Or that hanging out with Mr. Elhadad is not exactly my idea of a good time, but I nod anyway. "Sure."

By the time the evening call to prayer begins, the couch is finished, along with both beds, the dining room table, and three of the four dining chairs. Even though he's not very talkative, Adam Elhadad is very good with his hands. In a building furniture kind of way, I mean.

"Join us for dinner?" Dad asks Adam, who politely declines as Dad digs his wallet out of his back pocket. He thumbs through the bills and hands over several. "Thank you for your help."

"I can come again tomorrow in the evening, if you need me."

"That would be appreciated."

Mom thanks Adam in Arabic and he offers her a fleeting smile as he responds in kind. *"Afwan."*

"You know what would be great right now?" Dad says after Adam has gone. "Pizza. It's about a five-minute walk to the Pizza Hut."

"Casey, you gave that boy too much money," Mom says.

He shrugs. "I gave him next to nothing."

"We have to be careful here," she says. "If we give the Elhadads more money than they are used to having, they will get accustomed to having it. What happens when we leave and they have to go back to what they were earning before?"

"That's a harsh way to look at it, Beck."

"I'm being realistic."

"And I'm being altruistic."

Mom can't stop herself from smiling. "This is exactly why I fell in love with you, but we're going to burn through our savings if we aren't careful."

"We make more money than we spend," Dad says. "If we can't use it to make other people's lives better, what's the point of having it?"

She shakes her head, still smiling. "I hate it when you're right."

"You know what else I'm right about?" He rubs his hands together. "Pizza."

CHAPTER 4

*L*iving aboard a tugboat has made my dad impervious to thunderstorms. He can sleep through early morning lawn mowings and college football games on TV, so he is unaffected by the predawn call to prayer. Instead of trying to fight it, Mom and I sit on the new couch with the balcony doors open and just listen. In the dark, the call is haunting and I worry that I've absorbed some of Grandma Irene's fears.

When Dad told her we were moving to Egypt, she tried to get him to change his mind. She clipped out newspaper articles about suicide bombers. Brought over library books written by ministers and political talking heads about the dangers of Islam. Suggested I stay behind with her so I wouldn't be kidnapped. At the time it seemed like the exaggerations of a little old racist lady, but I would feel better if I understood the song coming from the minaret. Hopefully the difference between Grandma Irene and me is that I *want* to understand.

"It's not much different from church bells," Mom says, and I think about how all the churches in downtown Sandusky ring noon bells, slightly staggered and playing different melodies, but not unlike the calls to prayer. "In Arabic, the word for the call is *adhan* and the man who performs it is the *muezzin*. Each *muezzin* has his own style, which is why some calls are longer than others, but all of them are proclaiming that there is only one God, who is great, that Muhammad is the messenger of God, and—in this case—that prayer is better than sleep."

"That's it?"

"Basically. For Muslims the actual prayer comes next, but the *adhan* is simply a reminder that it's time to pray."

"They pray so much."

"I say prayers in the morning when I wake up and at night before bed, and we always say grace before dinner," she says. "If you count the moments when I am thankful for something good that happens or offer a prayer to ease someone's misfortune, it all adds up."

"Except your prayers are private."

"True, but this is what Islam requires," Mom says. "I'm sure there are plenty of Muslims who have trouble waking up for this prayer the same way you hate getting up early on Sunday morning for Mass."

It's not that I don't believe her, but the noon bells in Sandusky are more pleasant than the *adhan*. "I hope this means we'll eventually be able to sleep through it."

She ruffles my hair. "Me too. I'm tired."

When the call to prayer ends, we go back to bed, and when the real morning comes, Mr. Elhadad arrives to take us to Mom's new clinic. During the drive, she asks him about the neighborhood where the clinic is located.

"Manshiyat Nasr is called Garbage City," he says. "The people who live there—the Zabbaleen—collect the garbage from around Cairo and take it back to Manshiyat Nasr to sort out the recyclables. There is no running water there, no sewage system, and the electricity is almost nonexistent."

His description makes the place sound terrible, but he could not have prepared us enough for what we actually encounter. The neighborhood is a tightly packed warren of crumbling brick apartment buildings, and the mostly dirt streets are lined with bags of garbage. The air—which already stinks of Cairo smog—carries the sharp, sour stench of rotting food, and it takes all my willpower not to pull my shirt up over my nose. The children playing in the street, however, don't seem bothered.

We pass trucks stacked precariously high with bales of flattened water bottles, long-dead cars with smashed-out windows, and alleys filled with mountains of cardboard. Amid the garbage are wandering goats and vendor stalls selling fruits and vegetables. I don't think this was what Dad had in mind when he suggested we go in search of a market.

"It is easy to put this place out of our heads," Mr. Elhadad says, turning the car into a narrow street lined with shops. Overhead the buildings rise up ten stories and taller. Some of the balconies are strung with clotheslines pinned with drying laundry, while others have colorful fabrics creating privacy screens. "But it is a good reminder to be grateful for the blessings in our lives."

Dad shoots an *I told you so* glance over his shoulder at Mom, who sticks out her tongue at him, then smiles.

The clinic is at the end of a block, in a one-story building as dilapidated as the others, but someone has applied a fresh coat of blue paint over the stucco. My mother unlocks the front door. Inside the clinic is bright and clean with a small reception room, an even smaller office, and a couple of examination rooms. The space is ready. It's just waiting for equipment and staff. For Mom.

"How is this tiny place going to meet the needs of so many people?" Dad wonders aloud.

"It's not," she says. "But some is better than none."

The door opens behind us and a girl barely older than me comes in with a curly-haired baby on her hip. She says something in Arabic, gesturing at the baby. Mr. Elhadad responds, shaking his head. I don't understand their words, but I gather that he's telling her the clinic is not yet open.

"Wait," Mom says. "What's wrong? What does she need?"

"She says her daughter has sickness in her eye," Mr. Elhadad translates. "I believe she means infection."

My mom fishes a packet of peel-open latex exam gloves from her tote bag. As she pulls on the gloves, she speaks to the young woman in Arabic. I know Mom well enough to know she is asking permission to examine the baby, which is verified when the baby's mother nods her assent.

"She has conjunctivitis," Mom says in English. "She needs clean water, fresh toweling for compresses . . . I don't know how she is going to manage that in these conditions and I don't have the resources to help her today, but . . . okay, I'm going to need everyone to step outside so she and I can speak privately."

"What if you don't know the right words?" Dad asks.

"I'll improvise," she says. "This is personal. Between women."

As we wait outside, my dad buys a little of everything—oranges, tomatoes, a head of cabbage, broccoli, lemons, bananas, even a rutabaga—from a wrinkled old lady behind a wooden market stall that looks like it's one strong gust of wind away from toppling over. Mr. Elhadad watches, his mouth turned down in disapproval, as Dad doesn't bother trying to haggle. He probably gives the woman more than the asking price, too.

Mom comes out of the clinic with the young woman, who is smiling and saying *shokran* over and over.

"Did you get it all sorted out?" Dad asks.

"I did." Mom doesn't elaborate, but she is smiling too.

On the ride back to the apartment, I can't stop thinking about the girl in Manshiyat Nasr. I am fully aware that girls my age get pregnant all the time, but it's never happened inside my realm of experience. Most girls I know are still trying to figure out how to talk to boys, so the idea of being a married teenager—at least I assume she is married—with a baby boggles my mind. I can't help but wonder if she ever wishes for a life beyond Garbage City. Or maybe the Egyptian dream is different from the American dream. It's possible she has everything she wants.

The sun is high and the heat is suffocating by the time we arrived back at the apartment. In the elevator, I ask Mom what happened with the girl at the clinic.

"I gave her an unopened package of tissues from my bag and showed her the proper way to clean away the discharge," she says. "Then I told her as best I could, using gestures when necessary, that if she didn't have access to clean water, she should put a couple drops of breast milk in the baby's eye instead."

"Seriously?"

My mother nods. "It contains good bacteria, the kind that could help speed the healing process. It's a homeopathic thing and not proven science, but it's clean and, in this situation, better than using a questionable water source."

"You are so hard-core, Mom."

"This job . . ." She blows out a long breath and leans her head against Dad's shoulder. "It's going to be the hardest thing I've ever done."

CHAPTER 5

I try to respond to Hannah's e-mail, but I am not sure how to explain that Cairo is both better and worse than I imagined. The heat is like living under a blanket. The dust of the city sneaks in through every crack, every day. And it is never, ever quiet. I am not comfortable here—we've been in Egypt less than a handful of days, and my bedroom is the only place that even feels remotely "at home" even though everything in it still has that fresh-out-of-the-box smell.

My pink Kelleys Island stone sits on the nightstand beside a picture of Hannah, Owen, and me after Owen's conference final game. His dirty-blond hair was damp with sweat from playing almost the entire game and we were all holding up number one fingers. I am in a strange middle place tonight because my time in Cairo has only just started, but the picture makes me long for home. My fingers fly over the keyboard.

> *H—*
> *I've attached some pictures of my room and the*
> *view from our apartment and when I have more*
> *time, I'll try to tell you about Cairo. You can see*
> *how gorgeous it is where we live, but not every*
> *part of the city is like this. And this is not home.*
> *I miss you guys so much. Even if it's breaking the*
> *rules, tell Owen hi for me, okay?*
> *. . . and back,*
> *—C*

"Hey, Caroline." Dad's voice comes from the other side of my bedroom door. "Adam is here to help finish the furniture. We're coming in."

Before I can tell my dad that I need a minute to change, he barges in. My red Liverpool tank top and denim cutoffs would be totally appropriate at home, but here I'm all bare arms and legs in front of Adam. And when I look at him, he is staring at me. Our eyes meet for the briefest of moments and I see something raw there. Unguarded.

Adam Elhadad is checking me out.

His gaze drops as color rises in his face. He is not boy-next-door cute like Owen. The dark scruff along his jaw makes Adam seem older, more handsome than cute. His attention is flattering. Fluttering. Flustering. And I have no idea how to process this. I scoop up some other clothes and escape to the bathroom.

Could I be attracted to a boy like Adam Elhadad? Is that even allowed? Would my parents be okay with that? Would I be okay with that? Even after I'm covered by a blue floral tunic dress and rolled-up jeans, I don't have the answers. Avoiding my room, I tell Mom I'm going for a walk in the neighborhood.

"Do you have your phone?"

We stopped to buy mobile phones on the way back from Manshiyat Nasr because our US plans don't provide coverage in Egypt. The only people programmed into my new phone are my parents, Hannah, Owen (even though I'm not supposed to have him in there), and Mr. Elhadad. I pat my back pocket. "Got it."

"Be careful."

For the longest time, I stand in the vestibule, unsure of which direction to go. Masoud sits beside the elevator, puffing on a hookah pipe. His snowy beard makes him look old enough to be someone's grandfather, and he watches me with dark, judgmental eyes. Like he's just waiting for me to do something wrong.

There is a movie theater down the road, but I don't know if the films are in English or in Arabic, or how to ask for a ticket if the person behind the glass doesn't speak my language. The Nile looks cool and inviting, and I think maybe I could walk along the waterfront.

Back home in Sandusky, one of the best spots along the shoreline is Jackson Street Pier. Mostly it's a parking lot for the ferries that go to Kelleys, South Bass, and Pelee Islands, but just before sunset the locals start circling in their cars, jockeying for the good spaces to open up at the end of the pier. When the weather was nice, Owen and I would ride our bikes and feed stale popcorn to the gulls. If we took his car, he would cue up "our" playlist into the stereo and, invariably, we'd be making out before the sun even went down. Overwhelmed by the nostalgia, I text him: I miss you.

As soon as I hit send, I wish I could take it back. Owen doesn't deserve to be jerked around just because I am afraid to take my first solo step in Cairo. Tucking my phone away, I head down the sidewalk in the direction of the theater. At the very least, I can see what movies are playing.

"Hello there." An Egyptian man falls into step beside me.

He is in his late twenties with slicked-back dark hair, invasive cologne that makes my nose twitch, and a Manchester United jersey. I look down at his hands to see if he has flyers or something he's trying to sell me, but his hands are empty. Why is he talking to me? What does he want? "I think blond girls are very sexy."

My pulse ratchets up a notch and I glance around, looking for a friendly face—or maybe an escape route. I want him to leave me alone, but I am afraid of what might happen if I tell him so.

"You are beautiful like honey." He's so far into my personal space that I can feel his hot, smoky breath against my face. "Sweet."

What if this was what Grandma Irene meant when she talked about kidnapping? I think about running, but I have no idea which direction to run other than back toward the apartment. I don't want this creeper to know where I live.

"I'm meeting my boyfriend." My voice shakes and I hate having to lie. Girls shouldn't need boyfriends—fake or otherwise—to get guys to leave them alone, but I am almost to the theater, and trying to deflect him is not working. What if he follows me into the building?

"If you were my girlfriend, I would not permit you to go out in the streets dressed in such a revealing way." His tone has gone cold. "Have you no respect for yourself, provoking men like this?"

My top covers me from my neck to below my backside, my jeans are not tight, I am wearing no makeup, and my hair is tied up in a messy bun. More of his skin is showing than mine, but I'm the provocative one? And how did I go so fast from sexy to lacking self-respect? My fear turns to anger.

"Go away." I put as much force as possible behind my words. "Leave me alone."

The movie theater is right here, my imaginary boyfriend waiting for me inside, but this man has killed my desire to be out in public. I spin around on the sidewalk and run as fast as I can. I glance back to see if he is following, but he just stands where he is, shouting at me in Arabic. The language sounds ugly coming from his mouth and makes me feel as if I am the one who has done something wrong.

I don't wait for the elevator, instead sprinting past Masoud, up the stairs by twos, and rushing into the apartment. Only when the door is firmly closed behind me do I feel safe.

"Are you okay?" Mom asks as the afternoon *adhan* begins. Even with the windows closed and the air-conditioning on, there is no escaping the call to prayer. I can't help wondering if the man down in the street will stop to pray, wondering if his god approves of harassing women.

"I want to go home."

"What happened?"

"Some guy hit on me," I say. "And when I asked him to leave me alone, he basically accused me of dressing like a whore."

"This happens often in Cairo." Adam stands in the doorway of my room. "Some Egyptian men believe foreign women dress . . . I do not know the correct word . . . in such a way to attract attention."

"Nothing about *this*"—I motion toward my own body, but he glances away quickly, looking out the balcony doors—"is meant to attract attention. What am I supposed to do? Cover myself up like those ladies who only have their eyes showing?"

Adam's gaze swings back, meeting mine for a second. "It would not matter if you did. There are men who would harass the *niqabi* for wearing makeup on their eyes."

"That is so sexist."

He nods, but his shoulders lift a little at the same time. "My mother has been harassed, my sister even worse. There is not much that can be done. You must try to ignore it."

"That's easy to say when no one is questioning *your* self-respect." The anger in my voice earns me a sharp look from Mom and I wish I could reel back my words. I don't understand how Egyptians just let this kind of thing happen, but Adam isn't to blame for what happened to me. It's not his fault that harassment is an issue in his country.

"I am sorry." He sounds sincere. "The furniture is finished, so I should go. My father will be looking forward to your call if you should need him."

CHAPTER 6

It's about a week later when Mr. Elhadad knocks on our front door. Dad's back in the United States for work and Mom has spent the week training her staff, preparing the clinic for opening, and nagging me to get out of the apartment. After seven days of self-imposed exile, even cat videos are starting to lose their appeal and I am reluctantly ready for a day out with my personal driver.

Except when I pull open the door, Adam is standing in the hallway with damp curls and his hands shoved deep in the pockets of his jeans.

"Where's your dad?" I ask.

Just yesterday I was crunching my way through a bowl of Fruit Rings—the Egyptian equivalent of the American brand—when Mom issued her ultimatum.

"I am not going to let you spend the whole year hiding out in the apartment," she said. "Either you call Mr. Elhadad or I will."

"But—"

"No buts." Mom cut me off before I could point out the dangers, like creepy guys, the insane traffic that might run over me, or the fact that I know only one Arabic word. "Ahmed will be with you."

"Hanging out with someone else's dad," I muttered into my cereal bowl. "That should be fun."

Mom gave me her Dr. Rebecca Kelly Hulk Smash look—not unlike the one she gave the rental agent—and any other protests I might have had went down my throat with a mouthful of cereal. "I'm making the call."

She dialed Mr. Elhadad, whose enthusiasm boomed so loudly down the phone line I could hear him across the kitchen. "Tomorrow I will take her to the pyramids," he said. "It will be good fun. I will arrange a guide."

Disconnecting the call, my mom said, "I understand that Cairo can be a scary place—I go out into the city every day—but you have been given an opportunity most kids don't get. I won't let you waste it."

Now opportunity stands before me, looking less than thrilled to be here. "My father woke with a fever," Adam explains. "He sent me in his place."

"Is that okay?" I ask. "What about your job?"

He does his little shrug-nod combination, as if it's not actually okay but there is nothing he can do about it. "Someone will be happy to take my shift."

The space between his dark eyebrows is creased with worry, though. Am I putting his livelihood on the line?

"I can go another day," I offer. "When your dad is feeling better."

"My father's business is more important than my job. Today will be fine."

His dad's car is parked outside the building and Adam opens the door for me. It's strange to be sitting in the back, especially when there are only two of us in the car, but he seems intent on keeping as much space between us as possible. I don't know if it's a Muslim thing or an Adam Elhadad thing, but it makes me feel pretentious. As we stop-and-start through traffic over the Abbas Bridge into Giza, I pull out my phone to check the score of the Liverpool friendly summer game against a team from Australia.

Like most kids back home, I started playing recreational league soccer out at Osborn Park when I was five. Everyone gets a T-shirt and every team has at least one little kid (on my very first team it was Hannah) who spends more time picking clovers out of the grass than actually learning the game.

But it wasn't until I started dating Owen that I had a favorite professional team. His uncle Sean spent a college semester in England and sent back a Liverpool supporter's scarf as a gift for his nephew. I first liked the team because of Owen's obsession, but as I followed along for three years, they grew on me. Even when they're losing. Which they are right now.

"Oh, come on, Liverpool. Seriously?"

The games are usually on television early in the morning back home—six hours behind England—so Owen sometimes came over to watch with me. When he was home, Dad would join us, and Mom would make peanut-butter-and-banana French toast. The tears that come with the memory take me by surprise and I am wiping them on the sleeve of my shirt when Adam says, "You support Liverpool?"

Looking up, I catch a glimpse of his eyes in the rearview mirror as he waits for my answer. We are sitting in a veritable ocean of cars. Everyone is at a standstill.

"It's my own special brand of torture," I say. "But yes."

A smile wakes up his face, erasing the serious-lipped guy who walked into our apartment that first day. He is transformed. Not as intimidating. Adorable in a way that makes my heart beat a little bit faster. "They are my favorite too. An unpopular choice among my friends, who are all mad for United or City."

I crinkle my nose at the mention of the Manchester teams, earning a laugh. It is just one tiny, tentative thing, but for the first time since we met, we've made an actual connection. "Favorite Liverpool player?"

"Any?" Adam asks. "Or from the current squad?"

"Either."

"Pepe," he says, referring to the former goalkeeper. "Yours?"

"Gerrard."

Adam smiles again. "I was going to say Gerrard."

"I almost said Pepe."

He looks at me in the rearview mirror again, this time as if he is actually seeing me, and I realize what I miss most about home is not Owen; it's hanging out with people my own age. I want to see the pyramids with the people who are related to me, but I want to *talk* to someone who's not. "Hey, um— Adam?"

"Yes?"

"Do you think maybe we could do something else? It's just—I've been stuck in the apartment all week and I'm homesick, and today doesn't feel like the right day to see the pyramids."

He is quiet for a moment and then he nods. "I know what you need."

We are caught up in a current of cars committed to making a left turn, but Adam navigates across the lanes, amid the blaring horns of angry drivers. It is not unlike a salmon swimming upstream and I pinch my eyes closed, hoping we don't share the same fate as the fish, until we are heading straight. He falls back into silence and I'm not certain if it is because he's concentrating on driving—maybe it takes a lot of effort to be terrifying behind the wheel of a car—or if he's already said too much.

Finally he double-parks in front of a small restaurant tucked into the lower level of a sand-colored building, leaving the engine running. "Stay in the car. I will be back."

On my left, the passing traffic comes within inches of the sedan, and on the right, the owner of the car we double-parked next to shakes his fist at me, as if I am the one who boxed him in. Two minutes later Adam comes out of the restaurant with a plastic bag hanging off his fingers. He waves off the man—who is now shouting at him—and climbs back into the driver's seat. As we motor away, the scent of warm starch, tomatoes, and a note of vinegar fills the car.

"What did you buy?"

"You will soon see."

We end up back over the bridge on the island where I live. Adam drives past the apartment building and comes to a stop at a riverfront park just down the road. This time, though, he actually pulls into a parking space and kills the engine.

I follow him down the brickwork path into the park, where he selects a bench beneath the shade of a leafy tree with a view of the Nile. We sit on opposite ends of the bench and the bag between us rustles as Adam takes out two plastic tubs—the size of large margarine containers—filled with a mixture of rice, macaroni, spaghetti, lentils, and garlic, topped with a tomato sauce, and sprinkled with chickpeas and fried onions. It's like someone opened their pantry, dumped all the random leftovers into one pot, and called it dinner.

"*Koshary* is Egyptian comfort food," he explains. "I thought maybe it would help you to feel better."

"That was . . . really sweet. Thank you."

The *koshary* is both starchy and crunchy, and the sauce a little bit spicy. None of the flavors and textures should go together but they do, and I take another bite because it is—inexplicably—comforting.

"I cannot imagine moving so far from my home," Adam says. "Cairo must be a difficult place for you with the noise and the language and—"

"Bad drivers."

His laugh is low and quiet, the same way he talks. "If I were a bad driver we would have gotten into an accident, but we did not, so clearly you are mistaken."

"If you weren't stuck driving me around today, what would you be doing?"

"Making *koshary*."

"Really?" I poke my fork around in the plastic tub, looking for spaghetti noodles.

"In reality I clean tables, sweep the floors, and serve *koshary* to takeaway customers because I am an apprentice," Adam says. "But sometimes my boss allows me to do the cooking. Don't tell him, but my own *koshary* tastes better."

"That's a strong claim."

"Maybe one day I will prove it to you."

I'm not sure what to say because it seems like he is flirting with me, but Owen was my boyfriend for so long that my own skills are rusty. What if I'm wrong? What if Adam is just being a nice guy? Eventually, after thinking about my answer for far too long, I say, "Maybe."

As we eat, we watch the other people in the park. A young mother hovers as her toddler tosses pebbles into the river with chubby little fingers. Not far away, a young guy perches on a railing with a girl standing between his knees. His face is close to hers as they talk privately and a pang of melancholy cuts through me.

"Do you, um—do you have a girlfriend?" I ask, watching as the guy lays a gentle hand against the girl's cheek. He smiles at her as if she is his whole world. As my question hangs in the air, I worry whether it's an appropriate question to ask a Muslim guy I barely know.

"Relationships before marriage are not something Islam encourages. Some of my friends have girlfriends, but . . ." He trails off, leaving me to wonder what he was going to say. He's shy? Conservative? A jerk who can't get a girlfriend? I bite back a smile at the ridiculousness of that last thought. He knew what I needed even when I didn't. Adam Elhadad is definitely not a jerk.

"So if Muslims are not supposed to have relationships before marriage, how do you find someone to marry? Aside from breaking the rules, I mean."

"Friends. Family members. Sometimes parents will arrange the marriage."

I try to imagine my mom and dad picking out a husband for me, and I wonder if they would have picked Owen. "How do you know they'll choose the right person?"

"Who knows you better than your family?"

"Um . . . me?"

The corner of his mouth lifts. "Sometimes families do not choose well."

"So why not just date?"

Adam shifts a little on the bench, angling himself in my

direction. "Islam says the goal of any relationship should be marriage. Dating has the potential for sinful behavior."

One of the most embarrassing moments of my life was the time I was grocery shopping with Grandma Irene and she asked me if I was having sex with Owen. When I said no—which was the truth—she said, "Good, because premarital sex is a sin and you will go straight to hell." At that moment, I'd kind of wished a portal would open and drag me there, because hell could not have been worse than talking about sex with my grandma in the bread aisle at Kroger.

"There are some who believe the two of us sitting here alone is haram," Adam says.

"And haram is bad, right?"

He nods. "Right."

Over the course of my lifetime I've spent tons of time alone with boys. Luke Corso lets me bum a ride to school whenever my car is out of commission. Whenever I see Fernando Leal—a defender on the public high school soccer team—kicking around in the park between our houses, I'll go join him. And there have been countless times I've watched TV alone with any one of Hannah's brothers. None of those encounters led to anything remotely sinful. "Do *you* think what we're doing is haram?"

"I would not be here if I were not your driver, but . . ." He trails off as his shoulders lift and drop.

Maybe he's not thinking about marrying me, but buying a girl comfort food and taking her to a quiet park in the middle of a chaotic city are not listed in the job description. Also, now I'm pretty sure he's flirting with me, intentionally or otherwise. I nudge him with my elbow. "Good thing I'm the boss of you then, huh?"

He looks away, his expression inscrutable, leaving me to wonder if I've stuck my foot in my mouth. I was only joking, but what if Adam took it seriously? The crinkling of the plastic bag seems unnaturally loud as I pack away the empty *koshary* tubs. "I mean, I'm *not* your boss. I'm just—I, um—I should probably go. Since my house is just down the street, I can walk from here."

My face burns as I take my wallet from my purse, feeling as if I'm adding insult to injury. I hand him some bills. Hopefully enough to pay him back for lunch, as well as a respectful tip. I need to get better at Egyptian money, but more important, I need to figure out how not to crash through cultural boundaries. "Thanks for rearranging your life for me . . . and the *koshary* was exactly what I needed."

Adam says my name when I'm just a few steps away from the bench and the little roll of the *r* as it moves across his tongue makes me want to hear him say it several thousand times. I turn back as he catches up to me. "You'll never walk alone."

I crack up laughing at his perfectly timed, deadpan reference to the Liverpool anthem. "I hope your dad feels better soon," I say when we reach the car. "And thanks again. Today was nice."

His mouth softens and he offers a shy smile, along with a nod. "Yes. It was."

CHAPTER 7

I wait a few days before calling Mr. Elhadad again. Partly to give him time to recover, but mostly because having a driver makes me hyperaware of my privilege. My mother's driver has the legitimate task of driving her to and from Manshiyat Nasr, but Mr. Elhadad is saddled with an American teenager. A tourist, basically. Except when Dad calls from the tugboat and wants to know what fun things I've done in his absence, I have no answer.

The next day I ask Mr. Elhadad if he will take me to the souk at Khan el-Khalili, one of Cairo's most popular bazaars.

"Tomorrow my son will take you to the Friday Market." His voice is creaky from sickness. "The prices are much better."

"But—"

"He will come very early so you can arrive at the market before the crowd."

Mr. Elhadad hangs up before I can offer to wait until he feels better. I don't want Adam to have to shuffle his schedule for me again. He also leaves me wondering what the Friday Market might be—and how early is very?

With an entire day to fill, I decide to venture out alone again. I start out in the direction of the park but stop when I reach a tiny bakery. The sidewalk is half-obstructed by wooden racks piled with cooling loaves of fresh bread in different shapes and sizes, and the air around me smells yeasty. My stomach growls as I watch a woman buy several flatbreads, trickling coins into the bread seller's palm.

Their transaction complete, she walks away and I approach the man as I dig into my jeans pocket for some Egyptian coins. I point to a pita-style round and extend my hand to him, not knowing if what I have is enough or which coins are the right ones. The bread seller plucks a small bronze coin from the cluster—one that doesn't seem adequate for something homemade and fresh—and hands over the bread.

As I continue on my way, it hits me that both the bread seller and I touched dirty coins, then touched the bread. There is no bag. No nutrition label. Everything American in me says *don't eat this*, but it would be wasteful to throw it away, even if it was practically free. I tear off a bit of bread and shove it into my mouth. It's warm and delicious, and by the time I reach the park, both the bread and my worries are long gone.

I find a bench close to the river, where I sit and read my latest e-mail from Hannah.

> *C—*
>
> *I'm sorry it's taken me so long to write back. Your apartment is gorgeous and I am superjealous you have your own balcony, especially because it overlooks the freakin' Nile! You should buy some plants and maybe a big comfy chair to make your own little indoor/outdoor reading nook.*
>
> *Anyway, I think the full moon is making people crazy around here. Vlad (the Romanian guy from work) asked me if I would help him improve his English, so we've been kind of hanging out. And when we were at a party the other night at Emilee Yeager's beach, Owen was there with Jessie Roth.*
>
> *I have to get ready for work, but I'll write more soon. La revedere! (That's "good-bye" in Romanian.)*
>
> *Love you to the moon,*
>
> *—H*

Her letter creates more questions than answers. Particularly, why was Owen at a party with a girl when he claimed he didn't want to date other girls? I was the one who initiated the breakup and agreed to his terms, but it throws me that he's moved on so fast. I've only been gone two weeks. Except a little zing of pleasure runs down my spine whenever (which is often) I think about the way Adam Elhadad said my name, so maybe I'm being unfair. Jessie Roth is sweet and I want Owen to be happy. Still, if I returned to Ohio today, I'd want my boyfriend back.

The next e-mail is from Grandma Irene. With her, you never know what you're going to get. Some days she sends me videos of adorable baby goats and other days she sends me warnings about weird stuff, like how the colors in woven friendship bracelets supposedly have secret sexual meanings. According to Grandma's bracelet code, the blue-and-gold one I'm wearing now—the one Hannah made me in our school colors when we started as freshmen—apparently means I'm down for oral sex and hugging. (Only half correct.)

This e-mail is worse than her urban myths, though, because she asks me if I've met any nice American kids yet and urges me to stay away from Muslims. I'm in a country composed almost entirely of Muslims. I can't avoid them even if I wanted to do that, and it makes my stomach hurt when she says these things. No matter how often Dad tries to explain to her that her views are racist, she excuses herself by saying she is a product of a different era when people weren't so politically correct. I understand she's coming from a lack of understanding and a fear fueled by television news, but she is not too old to change. It's hypocritical to think going to Mass on Sunday excuses her from being racist the rest of the week. Shouldn't we be the same people all week long?

Finally, there's an e-mail from Uncle Mike because Grandma looped him into her warning about Muslims. She lives under a delusional cloud that because he was a career Marine, he shares her opinions. Instead he describes how he became close with a family in Tikrit, Iraq, on his last tour of duty. The family had small children who made him miss his own kids just a little bit less. When extremists regained control of the city after the US troops left, Uncle Mike had been beside himself with worry about that family, those kids.

"The vast majority of people you meet will treat you with kindness, especially since you're not carrying an assault rifle," he writes in his response to both me and Grandma. "Don't let fear hold you back."

Taking Uncle Mike's advice, I summon my courage and head down to the movie theater. As I walk, I look up Arabic numbers on my phone and practice them in my head: *wahid*, *itnayn*, *talata*, *arba'a*, *hamsa*, *sitta*. Eventually I should learn more, but there are six screens at this multiplex. Maybe knowing the first six numbers will help me order a ticket and find the right theater.

"Wahid," I say to the man behind the ticket window, then say the name of the film in English. It's a popular American book-to-movie adaptation, and to my relief, he knows what I'm talking about. I slide a few Egyptian bills through the opening, and my ticket spits out from the counter.

The lobby inside is plastered with posters of upcoming films, just like back home, and the snack bar sells overpriced candy and enormous tubs of popcorn. The ticket taker speaks to me in Arabic as he gestures to the right and I recognize *hamsa*. My movie is in theater five.

I get a few curious glances and too-long stares, but no one bothers me as I position myself in a row behind a group of teenage girls. The chairs are outdated but appropriately squishy, and the floor a bit sticky (so not all that different from my usual moviegoing experience, really). It is kind of strange to be going alone to a movie that I was planning to see with Hannah—even more strange to be seeing it in Cairo—but when the lights go down and the previews begin, I get lost. Just like everyone else.

CHAPTER 8

S o where exactly are we going today?" I slide into the car as Adam stands beside the open door. I still don't like sitting in the back, but it seems clear he is not ready to invite me up front. Also, when Mr. Elhadad said early, he wasn't joking. The sun is still really low in the sky.

"The souk al-Gomaa," Adam says. "It is not such a tourist place as el-Khalili and you will find better values. I can help you."

I studied up on the Khan el-Khalili. The heart of the marketplace is in an ancient mausoleum in the oldest part of Cairo, and the bazaar spiderwebs out through streets and alleyways filled with shops, coffeehouses, restaurants, and street vendors of every stripe. The pictures online capture the old stonework buildings, tables outside shops covered with shiny trinkets, doorways surrounded by rugs and tapestries, and colorful barrels of fragrant spices.

Al-Gomaa, as it turns out, is not the same at all. It's more like a garage sale on the surface of the sun. Very little shade and crowded shoulder to shoulder with locals—mostly men—looking to buy anything and everything. Clothing. Shoes. Appliances. Toys. Car parts. There are vendors who have blankets spread on the ground, covered with broken clocks and watches, selling for piastres—the Egyptian equivalent of pennies. Other vendors have tables filled with obsolete computers, bulky old-model TVs and VCRs, and row after row of cell phones—many of which, Adam says, might be stolen.

"Remind me why your dad thought this would be a good idea?" I ask as we squeeze past a man banging on a drum to advertise his air conditioners. I have a feeling the shops at Khan el-Khalili don't sell air conditioners or carburetors.

"At el-Khalili the prices are for tourists," Adam says. "But this is for Egyptians. It is not all good-quality merchandise and much of it is secondhand, but this is what many Egyptians can afford. If you look carefully you can find very nice things."

I'd have been content with tourist prices and a picture-perfect setting instead of mass chaos and feeling so very conspicuous, but I don't tell him that. Even when an anonymous hand slides across the back of my jeans and squeezes my butt. My fingers clench in self-defense but I don't know who to lash out against. I feel defenseless in this bustling sea of strangers.

Adam stops at a vendor selling furniture and chandeliers. "Maybe this is what you are looking for?"

Amid dusty old floral couches and antique dressers there's a tufted chair covered in fading pink velvet with gold-leaf legs. The kind of chair I imagined when Hannah suggested a reading nook.

"So what do I do when I want to buy something?" I ask Adam. "Because I like that chair."

"The thing you must remember is this—never be too eager and be confident," he says. "If the seller believes you will walk away from the sale, he will offer a better price. I will show you, but first you must decide how much you want to pay for the chair."

"I have no idea." Having never shopped for antiques in the United States, I have zero frame of reference as to how much a chair like that should cost. "No more than thirty dollars?"

"I will do what I can."

I step aside as Adam greets the stallholder and motions toward the chair. I don't understand a single word as they go back and forth, but they are both smiling, as if they are having a casual conversation instead of battling over a piece of furniture. Finally Adam nods and the two men shake on the deal.

"You have a chair," Adam tells me. "For two hundred Egyptian, which is about twenty-five American dollars. He will put a tag on it and we can pick up the chair on our way back to the car."

"Thank you."

As we wander through the market, I ask him about his family.

"You have met my father, obviously," he says. "His dream as a young man was to be a professor of English, but my grandparents were very poor so he could not attend university. Instead he learned English on his own so he could hire himself as a driver to the tourists and expatriates. He likes Americans very much."

We pause at a stall selling the same kind of brass hanging lanterns I'd seen in photos of the Khan. There are many styles I like, but this is something to buy on our way out of the market so we don't have to carry them around all morning.

"My mother is Manar and she works in a wedding shop, making alterations to dresses," Adam continues as we walked on. "And my sister, Aya, is fifteen. She is in high school, and, like my father, she dreams of going to university. I think she will be able."

"What do *you* dream?"

"I will be a chef," he says, and I love his quiet confidence.

"Sweeping the floors in a *koshary* shop is only the beginning."

Almost immediately I realize that if he were to ask me the same question, I would not be able to answer. I have the luxury of taking the time to figure out what I want to do with my life, of being able to afford college. I've never had to work to help put food on the table. In fact, working at Cedar Point with Hannah would have been my first job ever.

And then he asks.

CHAPTER 9

*W*hat about you, Caroline? What is your dream?"

I deflect with a laugh, trying to push away the guilt of having a life so easy that even my dream for the future can be deferred. "Breakfast."

We eat at an elaborate red-and-green wooden food cart with Arabic words carved into the side panels. Adam orders two of whatever the vendor is offering, and we watch as he ladles a bean mixture—kind of like refried beans, but not quite so pasty—into shallow metal bowls. He serves the bowls with bread that is very much like pita. "This is *fūl*," Adam explains, pointing to the beans. The word sounds like "fool" but longer in the middle. "It is made of fava beans with garlic, cumin, and onion. You use the *aish*—the bread—to scoop like so"—he dredges the pita through the beans—"and eat."

I pick up a pita and break off a small portion.

"So, in Egypt, we use our right hands to eat."

"Really? Why didn't you tell me that when we were eating *koshary*?"

"That was not important in that moment," he says. "But when you are Muslim, you use your right hand for all things honorable, such as eating, shaking hands, and preparing yourself for prayer. It is symbolic of the right hand of Allah."

"What happens if you're left-handed like me? I'm not sure I can eat without spilling food all over myself."

"When I was a very small boy, my mother tied my wrist to the chair so I was forced to use my right hand," he says. "Eventually I learned, but I still write with my left hand."

It makes me stupid giddy that we're both left-handed. "I bet you have an advantage writing Arabic, though."

Adam smiles. "Yes, no smudges on the side of my hand. But my father . . . when he was young, the teacher tried to make him use his right hand and then marked him poorly when he made the words badly."

"The same thing happened to my grandma Rose at Catholic school, and after her first bad grade, she refused to try again." I shift the pita to my right hand. "Okay, I'm going in."

"Because you are not Muslim, you can eat with any hand

you like, but I'm telling you this in case you are ever in the company of Muslims. It is proper etiquette."

"I don't mind. I'll try it."

After seventeen years of eating with my left hand, I feel like a toddler and the bean mixture drips down my wrist as I bring it to my mouth. The texture reminds me of hummus but is warm and almost nutty in flavor. Garlicky.

"This is heaven." My mouth is full and I don't even care about manners. "I like it even better than *koshary*."

"*Fūl* is a common breakfast food," Adam says. "My mother serves it with a fried or boiled egg."

"See, in the United States, we really don't eat beans for breakfast," I tell him. "We eat eggs and meat and lots of sweetened things like cereal, oatmeal, and pancakes. But I would totally eat this."

"I do not like to eat this very often because it is filling and makes me sleepy."

I tell him about my mom's peanut-butter-and-banana French toast. "Two or three slices and a nap is in my immediate future."

"I have never eaten French toast."

I smile. "Maybe I'll have to make it for you."

He ducks his head, focusing on his food, but not before I catch a hint of a grin and a barely audible "Maybe."

"So, yesterday, I bought *aish* by myself," I tell him. "And then I went to the movies alone."

Adam's eyebrows hitch up. "Is this so?"

"I've never really done that before, not even back home," I say. "But I kind of enjoyed being alone. Is that weird?"

"My friends, at the movies, are always talking so much," he says. "Sometimes I go alone, so I do not think it is weird."

"Maybe—" I stop myself from asking if he might want to see a movie with me sometime; it feels like a step too far. Adam is here as a stand-in for his dad.

"What were you going to say?" he asks.

"Nothing important."

Adam returns the plates to the cart, then leads me to a stall where a young man pushes long stalks of sugarcane into a machine and extracts the juice. Adam orders two, and we watch as the juice funnels into a pitcher, which the vendor pours into plastic mugs. The liquid is pale green and a little frothy on top, and as Adam hands me a mug, I am not sure I want to try it.

"It is refreshing on a hot day," he says.

"So basically every day?"

He laughs. "In the summer, yes, but you would be surprised to know that Egypt can be cold in the winter."

I take a tiny sip of the juice and the first flavor to touch my tongue reminds me of the way grass smells when it's freshly cut, followed by a sweetness that is neither syrupy nor heavy. "This tastes like . . . well, if green had a flavor, it would taste like this."

"I have never thought about colors having flavors." Adam considers. "But I think you are correct. Green."

Like at the *fūl* cart, we have to give back the cups, so we drink the juice quickly.

"There is something else I think you might like to see." He leads me to a row of vendors selling nothing but animals. There are cages filled with all kinds of different birds—cockatoos, lovebirds, finches, cockatiels, parrots, budgies, chickens, geese, pigeons—but there are also dogs, goats, snakes, donkeys, and goldfish. I pause at a cage of lovebirds, watching a pair groom each other. I love their sweet red faces and I think about buying one, but I'm not sure how my parents would feel about that. I've never had a pet.

The vendor says something to us in Arabic.

"He asks if you wish to buy a bird," Adam translates.

"Maybe, but not today."

We move off through the market and he scores good deals for me on a couple of tapestries, a pair of scarves, some house-plants, and a junky-but-ornate old mirror that will look great with a coat of paint. We go back for three of the lanterns and return to the furniture stall to collect the chair. Arms loaded, we head to the car.

"You did very well today," Adam says as he ties the trunk lid down around the chair, which doesn't quite fit all the way.

"No, *you* did very well."

"I am sure my father would be happy to teach you a few bargaining phrases."

I feel a little deflated by the suggestion. Not because I don't want to learn to haggle for myself but because hanging out with Adam has been fun. Spending time with his dad, while maybe more appropriate, won't be the same.

As we drive back to Manial, I share with Adam the way his father frowned when Dad paid full price for the fruits and vegetables in Manshiyat Nasr.

"I'm certain he was disappointed," Adam says. "He loves to haggle and lives to win, but I am sure the woman was happy to receive your father's kindness. He seems to have a big heart."

Masoud lends a hand as we carry my new treasures up to the apartment, his eyes flitting suspiciously back and forth between Adam and me, as if he thinks he is the only thing keeping us from making out on the elevator floor. Warmth rises to my cheeks at the thought of making out with Adam anywhere.

"Thanks again for rescheduling your life for me, but I think I'll wait for your dad to get better before I call again," I say after everything is inside and Masoud is finally gone. "I

73

mean, you've got a kitchen to conquer and I definitely don't want to stand in the way of a dream."

Adam's face softens into a smile that burns itself into my brain, an image that resurfaces as I hang the largest tapestry on the wall behind the couch and as I position my new chair beside my balcony door.

"This is such a great start," Mom says when she comes home and sees the lanterns hanging in a cluster in the corner of the living room and the plants perched on the sunny end table.

I tell her about al-Gomaa, about trying *fūl* and drinking cane juice. What I don't tell her is that I'm kind of disappointed that I won't get to hang out with Adam Elhadad again.

CHAPTER 10

Wake up!" Mom sings as she flickers my bedroom lights to wake me up. The sun has barely cracked the horizon. "Mr. Elhadad will be here soon. Today's the day we're going to the pyramids!"

I wonder if Adam might come in his father's place again, but not long after I take a quick shower and eat an even quicker breakfast, Mr. Elhadad arrives. He looks a little tired around the eyes but otherwise recovered.

"It's nice to see you," Mom says as he opens the car door for her. "How are you feeling?"

"Much better, but the more important question is how the good work at your clinic is going."

My mother shakes her head. "Every day brings a new challenge. Yesterday, for instance, an elderly man brought his wife in for cataract surgery. It's a simple procedure that takes about fifteen minutes. When I finished with her, I asked him if he would like the surgery—his eyes were clouded worse than hers—but he refused and there was nothing I could say to get him to change his mind."

"This is not uncommon, especially with older and more conservative Muslims," Mr. Elhadad says. "These men believe that being examined by a woman doctor, allowing her to touch them, is *fitnah*—giving temptation the opportunity to occur. Only if there is no male doctor available is it permissible to see a woman."

Mom stifles a laugh with her hand. "I'm sorry. We're talking about medical conditions here. There is nothing sexy about cataracts."

Mr. Elhadad chuckles. "I understand, but this is what some people believe."

"And I understand that," Mom says. "It's just frustrating to deal with men who would choose to stay blind when they have a chance to see. I am not leading anyone into temptation, only using the talents God gave me."

The driver offers a sympathetic smile in the rearview mirror. "Be assured there are many Muslims whose minds are more open, but you will remain frustrated if you allow yourself to think this way. In Egypt? Better to hire a male doctor and move forward with your work."

"Yes," she says. "I supposed you're right."

"Now," Mr. Elhadad says as we reach the outskirts of Giza. "I must warn you that there are many touts offering camel and horse rides, souvenirs and such, and they can be very aggressive. Do not accept anything from them or they will demand payment. Nothing is free. And do not believe the only way to reach the pyramids is on the back of an animal. It is a long walk, but you may choose to walk."

Despite his warning, we are not prepared when a man comes running up alongside the car—before we've even reached the parking lot—knocking on the window and trying to open the door, all the while shouting, "Best camel ride! Best camel ride!" I slide closer to my mom as Mr. Elhadad speeds up, forcing the man to release his hold on the door handle.

"I have arranged a guide for you." The driver pulls into the parking lot. "So I am hoping his presence will keep the touts away, but the best method is to avoid eye contact with them and just say no."

The pyramids are closer now—more enormous than I could ever have imagined—and the sheer magnitude makes my breath catch in my chest.

Just then a group of young men on horseback thunders past, glossy black tails streaming out behind the horses as they gallop. A younger boy—maybe twelve or thirteen—runs after them with a riding crop in his hand, cracking it as hard as he can against the last horse's rump until the horses outpace him and he falls behind, laughing.

"If you would like to ride," Mr. Elhadad says. "Look for horses or camels that appear to be healthy and without sores. Your guide can make arrangements."

Simply walking to the ticket building is a gauntlet of pressure pitches. On both sides of us are tables filled with trinkets: pyramid-shaped paperweights, gold-plated pharaoh busts, and head scarves so tourists can look like Bedouins. Men offer us bottled water, boys offer to take our picture. They are relentless.

"For free," one man says, attempting to stuff a kaffiyeh into my hand, even though I am already wearing a baseball cap to keep the sun from incinerating my face. I curl my fingers into a tight fist so he can't make me take the scarf. "For a beautiful lady."

The thing is, even though I know it's not actually free, I still want the scarf in the same way I wanted a sand dollar painted with a tacky-looking sunset when I was five in Florida, or the Niagara Falls snow globe when I was eleven. Except I am afraid that to even talk to this man, let alone try to haggle with him, will open the floodgates to every other tout on the Giza Plateau. I shake my head and keep walking.

Our tour guide, wearing a KEEP PORTLAND WEIRD T-shirt, is waiting for us just outside the ticket building. "I'm Tarek Kamar," he says, his accent as American as mine as he shakes hands with both Mom and me. "Welcome to Egypt."

As we walk through the scorching heat, Tarek explains that he is an Egyptian American, born and raised in Detroit, studying at the American University in Cairo. "My grandparents live here, so I'm staying with them while I work on my Egyptology degree."

"How do you like it?" Mom asks.

"I love it now, but at first I was kind of overwhelmed," Tarek says. "I mean, Detroit's a big, dirty city, but not this big and not this dirty. And back home, without a mosque on every other street corner, it's pretty easy to skip out on prayer time."

"And now?"

He gives a small, embarrassed laugh. "I'm still pretty slack and my grandma is none too happy about that."

Tarek begins his tour, explaining that the pyramids are part of a vast complex of temples, causeways, and tombs of ancient wives and Egyptian nobles, as well as cemeteries where the people who built the pyramids were buried. I didn't have any of those things in my elementary school diorama. "So the three largest—the ones everyone thinks of when they think of the pyramids—are Khufu, Khafre, and Menkaure, all of whom were pharaohs during the fourth dynasty, around 2500 BC. The interesting thing . . ."

The trinket vendors fall away as we focus our attention on our guide, who tells us how the three largest pyramids align with the stars of the constellation Orion, which scholars believe was deliberate because Orion was associated with Osiris, the Egyptian god of rebirth and the afterlife; how more than two million stones were used to build Khufu, the Great Pyramid; and how the surface of the pyramids were once covered with polished white limestone that made them shine. The walk is long, just like Mr. Elhadad said, but Tarek fills the time with so many interesting facts.

"Whoa." The word whooshes out of me as we reach the base of the Great Pyramid. If it was breathtaking from a distance, it is mind-blowing up close. I lean back to look at the top. From this angle, it appears to go on forever, and the passing clouds make it seem as if it could topple over on us, even though centuries of existence say otherwise.

"We can go inside if you want," Tarek says. "It's basically a very narrow and hot passageway to the main chamber. I've taken people who think it's an Indiana Jones experience not to be missed, while others wished they'd saved their money. Your mileage may vary, but this time of year it will be superhot. Honestly, as cheesy as it seems, riding a camel over to the Sphinx is a lot more fun."

"I'm not sure I like how the animals are treated around here," Mom says.

"There are some pretty shady operations," he says. "Desperate circumstances make people do desperate things for money, but I found a guy I trust and we worked out a deal. I bring my business solely to him, he gives me a fair price, and no hassles over taking pictures."

Mom looks at me. "What do you think?"

Which is how I end up on the back of a camel named Sylvester Stallone.

CHAPTER 11

I was about nine or ten—and going through a horse-crazy phase—when Dad took me to a riding stable a few times. Riding a camel is nothing at all like being on horseback. First, the saddle is wider and longer with no stirrups, so I hang on for dear life, trying not to fall off the camel's back as he lifts up on his spindly legs. Second, the camel walks with an uneven, bumpy gait that makes it hard to predict which direction the next step might jolt me.

But as the camels caravan their way through the desert in a straight line, I finally relax enough to ease my grip on the saddle and take pictures of the pyramids, Amjad the camel man, and my mother, bumping along on a camel called Marilyn Monroe. Total tourist. I snap a shot of Sylvester Stallone's sand-colored ears and, after we dismount at the

Sphinx, take a photo of his grumpy camel face with gnarly teeth almost smiling at me—or trying to bite me. It's hard to tell for sure.

"So what did you think about the camels?" Tarek asks, leading us to the Sphinx. Like the pyramids, I didn't realize just how massive the statue was until now, as I find myself dwarfed by one of the enormous paws.

"It was pretty fun," I say, positioning myself next to Mom so Tarek can take our picture. "But I do kind of wonder what it would have been like to go inside a pyramid. Maybe I'll do that another day."

"Since you're going to be here for a year, my suggestion is to wait until the heat breaks," he says. "And then go to the Red Pyramid in Dahshūr. Same experience, fewer crowds."

We walk around the entire statue, and Tarek explains that the most common belief among Egyptologists is that the face of the Sphinx was meant to represent Pharaoh Khafre. "Some theorize that the Sphinx was built before the pyramids in the shape of a lion and was altered to look like a pharaoh at a later date. But the layers of rock match the layers of other structures during Khafre's reign, which suggests he was the one who built it. No one truly knows for sure, and I think we could study the plateau for another millennium and never have all the answers. It's fun to try, though."

Mr. Elhadad is waiting for us in the parking lot closest to the Sphinx when we finish taking pictures and say good-bye to Tarek.

"So why did you recommend an American instead of an Egyptian guide?" Mom asks as we tumble into Mr. Elhadad's car, slightly sunburned and hungry.

"Tarek is Egyptian. Perhaps he does not need the money so much as the locals, but he understands that customer happiness comes before baksheesh." Mr. Elhadad rubs his fingers together in a gesture many Egyptians use to indicate they want a tip for their services. "I was this way once, but Tarek taught me about TripAdvisor and I have changed. If people are happy with Tarek, they will be happy with me, and good reviews bring new customers to us all. Maybe this is not the Egyptian way, but one day my children will be married and I want to have the money for their weddings."

Since I was born, my parents have been putting money into my college fund. They've never once discussed saving money to pay for a wedding. "What about college?" I ask.

"There is no cost for university in Egypt," Mr. Elhadad explains. "When I was young, my family could not afford to live without my income, so I was unable to attend university. My wife, my son, and I have worked hard so Aya may go."

I know my family would make those kinds of sacrifices for

each other, but we've been lucky that we've never had to do it. I can't help thinking about the intense pressure that Aya must be facing. The first to go to college. The expectation that she will succeed. I glance at my mom, whose eyes seem to reflect what I've been thinking. She reaches over and gives my hand a squeeze.

On our way through Giza, Mr. Elhadad suggests we stop for a snack, and I am not even slightly surprised when he stops at the *koshary* shop where Adam works.

The restaurant is shabby yet opulent, with crystal chandeliers and a tiered fountain in the middle of the dining room. Kind of over-the-top for a place that sells *koshary*, but it is packed with people. Some wait for their orders at the long takeaway counter, while others are seated in the dining room.

Adam stands behind the counter, dressed like an actual chef as he dishes *koshary* with assembly-line speed from a huge metal bowl into the plastic takeaway tubs. His efficiency is impressive, and the way his eyebrows pull together as he concentrates makes me smile. I watch him work until my mom elbows me and I turn away to find the waiter standing at the table, waiting to take our order. Mr. Elhadad wears a curious expression, as if he has discovered a secret about me, and I wonder if maybe he has. The heat that creeps up the back of my neck makes me think so.

Unlike the day Adam ordered *koshary* to go, the waiter brings us plates of pasta and lentils with side dishes of chickpeas, onions, and tomato sauce so we can mix our own proportions. There are also small dishes of garlic oil and spicy pepper sauce.

"It's comfort food," I say, and a look of wonder crosses my mother's face. I like having this bit of local knowledge, even though I am still very much a stranger in Cairo. It might be a small thing, but it's another step forward. I choose more pasta and chickpeas, fewer lentils, to make my own custom *koshary*.

Mom takes a tentative bite as Mr. Elhadad tucks in a bigger mouthful. "My wife would not be pleased to know I am eating *koshary* because she worries I eat it too often, but we will not tell her, okay?"

"Your secret's safe with us," my mom says.

I wonder if Adam might come over to say hello, but the restaurant is constantly busy. As we pass the takeaway counter on our way out, Mr. Elhadad calls out a greeting to his son. Adam raises a quick hand to wave at his father and surprise registers in his eyes when he notices me. He doesn't wave to me—his attention turns immediately back to his work—but this time I don't take it personally.

"He is a hard worker," his father says, the pride thick in his voice, as we get back in the car. "I think one day he will be a great chef."

After the sun, food, and trekking around in the desert heat, I am ready to go home for a nap. Mr. Elhadad starts the ignition, then pauses, placing a hand on his chest.

"Are you okay?" Mom asks.

"Just a bit of indigestion." Sweat trickles down his temple and he fishes a handkerchief from his pocket to wipe it away, laughing. "My punishment, I think, for wanting to keep the *koshary* secret from my wife."

"Are you feeling any discomfort in your chest? A squeezing sensation?" Mom asks. "Indigestion is sometimes a symptom of a heart attack."

"No, no, no, it's nothing so dramatic—" His words drop off as he draws in a sharp breath. "Or perhaps I am wrong."

"Should we call an ambulance?" I ask.

"Too much traffic," Mr. Elhadad gasps. "An ambulance is no good."

I throw open the car door.

"I'll be right back," I call out as I run back toward the shop. Adam looks up as I come in alone. "Your dad is having a heart attack," I say. "We need you to drive."

He says something in Arabic to another man behind the counter, who gives a quick nod of assent. Adam rushes out from behind the counter, shoves his way through the crowd, and runs to the car. Mom has helped Mr. Elhadad into the backseat and is instructing him to chew an aspirin tablet as Adam flings himself behind the wheel. The doors are barely shut behind us when he pulls out into traffic, cutting off another car and earning an angry, prolonged honk.

From the front seat I look into the back, where Mr. Elhadad has released the top button on his shirt. His face is pale and sweat rolls down his cheeks, but Mom has her hand wrapped around his. I know from experience that she is telegraphing reassurance, helping him feel calmer. That's her superpower, even when there is nothing else she can do.

"We'll find you a male doctor when we get to the hospital," she teases, keeping her tone light and a smile on her face. "But for now you are stuck with me."

"Adam is a terrible driver," I add. "So it won't take long."

Mr. Elhadad gives a weak laugh. "With this team looking after me, I have nothing to fear."

CHAPTER 12

_M_r. Elhadad is sitting up when we arrive at his hospital room a couple of days later. We brought him to the emergency room in time and the heart attack was not severe, but the doctor decided to admit him for a few days of observation. Mr. Elhadad still looks a little pale and tired, but he is smiling.

"Is this a good time?" My mother holds up an old Steve McQueen movie on DVD and a box of really nice chocolates. "We come bearing gifts."

"Oh yes," Mr. Elhadad says, beckoning us forward. "Please come in."

Sitting in a chair beside the bed is his wife, wearing a long heather-gray dress with a red hijab, and in a second chair is a girl who glances up from her cell phone as Mom and I enter the room.

Mr. Elhadad introduces us, explaining that Mom saved his life. It could be argued that Adam's insane driving probably had more to do with it, but his wife looks so happy to see my mother.

"Thank you," Mrs. Elhadad says, hugging Mom.

They launch into conversation—a little English, a little Arabic—as Aya and I size each other up. She has the same dark eyes as her father. Her mustard-yellow maxi dress, faded denim jacket, and leopard-print hijab that matches her shoes are seriously cute.

"I like your outfit," I say.

She smiles. "I was thinking the same about yours."

The backs of my knees are sweating inside the rolled-up jeans that I paired with a navy paisley mini-dress. I don't know how Aya can stand wearing so much clothing. Maybe living under the Egyptian sun her entire life has made her immune to the heat, because her makeup doesn't look like it is melting off her face the way mine does. "Thank you."

"I am excited to meet you. My father says only that you are a girl about my own age." She speaks slowly, maybe because she's translating Arabic to English in her head first. Which is impressive in itself. English is a complicated language. "And Adam tells me nothing, no matter how often I ask."

"There's really not much to know," I say. "But Adam didn't

say much about you, either. Only that you're hoping to go to college."

"Yes," she says. "I would like to study engineering, inshallah."

"What is inshallah?"

"If it is God's will."

Grandma Rose has a favorite saying that goes: "If the good Lord is willing and the creek don't rise," which sounds similar to inshallah, albeit a little more colloquial. But it really brings to mind the part of the Lord's Prayer where we say "thy will be done." Either way, Christian or Muslim, it seems like we all hope we're on the same page with God.

"Inshallah, then."

"Thank you." Her smile grows, dimpling her cheek. "Will you go to university too?"

"Yes," I say. "But I haven't applied to any schools yet—I'll be doing that this fall—and I'm not sure what I want to study."

Aya's eyes widen. "You do not have to choose a program?"

"Well, some people know what they want to study, but others wait to decide on a major until after they've taken some classes," I explain. "I've been thinking about anthropology, but I've also considered sociology and communications. So I think I'll wait and see."

"You are fortunate," she says. "Here, your test scores decide which areas of study are open to you. If you meet the score of your preferred subject, you have a better chance of being placed in that program."

"What if you don't get your preferred subject?"

"Then that is also God's will," she says. "But if I work very hard and score high on the exam, there is a strong chance I will not be disappointed."

I'm glad I don't have to leave my future to fate, but if this is how it's done in Egypt, I admire Aya for rolling with it when she could be freaking out. "That sounds like a good plan."

She says something to her parents in Arabic and Mrs. Elhadad's light brown eyes—just like Adam's eyes—appraise me. It feels as if she is judging me, and I wonder if her husband told her about the way I stared at their son in the *koshary* shop. My face grows warm under her scrutiny, but then she nods.

"There's a McDonald's just next door," Aya says. "I asked if you and I might go there together for a drink."

"I'd like that."

Mom and I walked from our apartment, which is just down the block from the hospital. She says, "I'll see you at home."

Outside, with our parents left behind, Aya says, "I hope this is not too personal to ask, but I have never met an American girl my own age before. Do you have a boyfriend?"

"I did," I say. "But we broke up before I moved."

"Did you kiss him?"

There were nights when Owen and I kissed for hours, until our lips were puffy and our tongues were sore. There were other times—not nearly as often—that his hand would creep under my shirt while we were making out. The answer is more complicated than a simple yes or no, but I tell her yes.

She sighs. "Was it like the Nicholas Sparks movies?"

I laugh out loud, then feel bad when her smile slips. "Not exactly. I mean, Owen and I were fourteen the first time we kissed. His mouth crashed against mine and our teeth bumped, which was kind of . . . painful. Eventually, though, we totally learned how to kiss like in the movies."

It's not the whole truth because sometimes Owen's tongue had a mind of its own and a heart set on my tonsils. He kissed like a teenage boy instead of a movie star, but Aya's smile reappears, so I let her enjoy the fantasy.

Just before we reach McDonald's, a group of boys around our age comes toward us. The one in the lead pushes his way between us and says something to Aya that makes the other boys snicker. One of them trails his fingertips down my braid as he passes and I curl my fingers into my palm to keep from slapping his hand away. My heart races as I take Aya by the arm, pulling her into the restaurant as the boys move on, jostling each other and laughing.

"What did he say to you?"

"Something I would not like to repeat," she says.

Once, when I was twelve, I was walking home from school when I reached a busy intersection. I started across just a few minutes too late and the light changed when I was about midway. I jogged the remaining steps and when I reached the opposite curb, the guy in a waiting car clapped and yelled, "Nice tits," as he drove away. I don't know any girl who doesn't have a similar story, but mostly they are isolated incidents, not an unrelenting part of our everyday lives. "How do you deal with this?"

"There is nothing I can do to stop it," Aya says. "I fear speaking out will make it worse. So I try to ignore and pray that Allah will judge them with the fairness they deserve."

"Guys like that deserve to have their dangly bits snapped off by crocodiles."

Her voice is low, her mouth behind her hand, when she says, "Sometimes I pray for that, too."

The restaurant resembles just about every other McDonald's restaurant I've ever visited, but the menu items are listed in both Arabic and English, and the girls behind the counter wear tan hijabs that match their uniform baseball caps. The menu also offers Chicken Big Macs and McArabia sandwiches with *kofta* patties—basically flat meatballs—folded into pita bread. It reminds me of the McRib sandwiches back home, which Hannah always called the McWhy—"Why get it at McDonald's when it would taste better literally anywhere else?"

The memory brings a smile to my face, and as Aya orders a McChicken sandwich and a kiwi-flavored drink, I pull out my phone so I can show her a picture of my friends in Ohio. Then I remember this is my Egyptian phone. I have photos of the Nile, the park across from the apartment, and from the Friday Market—even a picture of her brother haggling for a chair— but no pictures of Hannah or Owen. Instead I snap a picture of the menu board to share with Hannah later.

"As I said before, I am a romantic," Aya says as we choose a table near the window. "I know the Sparks movies are not real, but they make me feel like such a love is possible. I trust my family to choose a good husband for me, but I would rather find a love match myself. Perhaps at university."

"What if he wasn't Muslim?" I ask, unwrapping my double cheeseburger. It looks the same as the American version. I test-drive a french fry. Tastes the same.

Aya shakes her head. "No."

"No?"

"My parents are very open-minded compared to many people of their generation," she says. "But this would be too much for them. Muslim women may only marry Muslim men."

"Does that mean—never mind."

"What?"

"Nothing."

She studies me for a moment. "Were you going to ask about my brother?"

"No."

Maybe I say it too quickly, but the corner of her mouth tilts in a way that suggests she doesn't believe me.

"The rules are different for men," Aya says. "It is preferred they marry Muslim women, but they are allowed to marry Christians or Jews. His wife does not have to convert to Islam, but their children must be Muslim. But if we are talking about my brother, I think my mother would not want him to marry someone outside our faith."

"I don't want to marry your brother," I say, my eyes on my sandwich instead of her, so embarrassed that it feels like my face might burst into flame.

"But maybe you would like to kiss him?"

"Oh my God. No."

Aya laughs so hard I think she might slide off her bench onto the floor. "I'm sorry. I should not tease you. I understand my brother is very good-looking—some of my friends think so—but all the time he is cooking, cooking, cooking, and nothing turns his head."

"Yeah, he seems really focused on becoming a chef."

"It is better that way. Men are supposed to save up their money and establish households for their wives before they get married."

"That's a long time to be alone."

Aya shrugs. "We have our families, friends, work, prayer, and Allah. We are not alone."

She has a point, but it still seems out of sequence to me. Aren't all those things made better with love? My parents dated enough people to know they were right for each other. They saved their money together. Worked together to make a home—for themselves and for me.

Rather than giving voice to those thoughts, I take a bite of my burger, and everything tastes . . . not wrong, exactly, but the meat, the cheese, the ketchup, even the pickles, taste different. McDonald's is the one place in Egypt where I expected consistency, but it's another adjustment I have to make. I put down the sandwich and look at it for a moment, as if it might miraculously conform to my American standards. Then I pick it back up for another bite.

CHAPTER 13

Hannah's face appears on my computer screen and the first thing I notice is the new blond streak in her dark hair. It looks really cute and I tell her so. She pulls the pale color—about the same shade as my hair—through her fingers, and I feel a little sad that she dyed her hair without me.

"I finally talked my mom into letting me do it," she says.

Mrs. Gundlach is pretty old-fashioned about . . . everything. Hannah wasn't allowed to get her ears pierced until she was sixteen, her school uniform skirt has always been hemmed exactly to the dress-code regulation length (which is why Hannah always wears pants to school), and her mom would probably disown her if she even *thought* about getting a tattoo. Permission to put a blond stripe in her hair is a huge victory for Hannah.

"Jess helped me with the color," she says. "And I have to put it back to normal before school starts."

"That's, um—" Bitterness lodges in my chest like a pebble in a shoe. Between Hannah and Owen, it feels as if I have been replaced by Jessie Roth. "That's cool."

"She's not you," Hannah says quickly. "It's just—"

"I get it. We can't freeze time until I get back." I smile. Change the subject. "How's the Romanian boyfriend?"

"He's not—" She glances away shyly with a little smile tugging at the corners of her mouth. On a computer screen it's hard to tell, but it looks like she might be blushing. "I don't know how it happened, Caroline. On the first day Vlad was this cute-but-I-cannot-be-bothered-with-this-language-barrier-thing-right-now guy, but working together every day, talking all the time . . . he just kind of grew on me."

"So have you been on actual dates and stuff?"

"I guess Emilee's party was our first real date," Hannah says. "But before that we spent a whole afternoon watching movies in his dorm room. He likes to read what the people on the screen are saying. It helps with his English."

"Your mom's okay with you dating him?"

"He ticks all her boxes," she says. "Clean-cut. Polite. And he's Catholic. She actually invited him over for dinner."

With five siblings, dinner at Hannah's house can be

overwhelming. Two of her younger brothers—both wrestlers—are eating machines, while the youngest is still working on his hand-eye coordination when it comes to using utensils. It isn't safe to sit near any of them.

"If he survived your family, he's gotta be brave."

Hannah laughs. "Right? But he has a big family too, so he gets it."

"Have you kissed him yet?"

"Maybe."

"Hannah!"

"Okay. He kissed me after I drove him back to the dorms the night he came for dinner," she says. "He definitely knows what he's doing. But we won't tell my mom about that."

Adam comes to mind and I wonder if he's ever kissed a girl. Dating might be against the rules, but maybe kissing is a rule he's broken.

"I hate to ask," I say to Hannah. "But what happens when the summer ends?"

"I'm trying to live in the moment and just enjoy it, you know? I don't really want to think about that."

"Check it out." I stand up and angle my laptop away from me, so she can see the new chair. Mom found a DIY recipe online for cleaning velvet, which not only woke up the color but banished the old-chair smell.

"Perfect," Hannah says. "Where did you get it?"

I tell her all about my visit to the Friday Market as I pan the computer slowly around the room, explaining that Adam scored deals on everything that wasn't from IKEA.

"Wait. Who's Adam?"

"Okay, so the thing about Cairo is that the traffic is nuts and I don't have a driver's license, so when I need to go somewhere, I have a driver." I settle back in front of my computer. "Adam's dad is my regular driver, but he's been sick lately, so Adam took over a couple of times. He also helped my dad build the furniture."

"Is he cute? Or is he all beardy?"

"What does that even mean?"

"I don't know." Hannah shrugs. "My only frame of reference when it comes to the Middle East is Osama bin Laden."

"He was a terrorist."

"I didn't mean it like that. I just thought all the dudes there had beards."

"The Middle East is a huge place—a bunch of different countries that have their own cultures. Not all the men have beards, just like not all the women wear hijabs, but misconceptions like these are how people end up believing that everyone from the Middle East is a terrorist."

"I don't think that! Caroline, you know I don't think that!"

"Just making sure."

An awkwardness settles over us, but I push through it, hitting send on a picture I took of Adam haggling at al-Gomaa. "Anyway, being cute and having a beard aren't mutually exclusive, but Adam does not have a beard and he is very cute."

"Very? I feel like you're leaving something out of this story."

"There's nothing to tell, Hann. He's Muslim."

"Ooh! Forbidden romance."

"No romance."

My e-mail dings in her in-box and Hannah gasps. "Oh my God! He has Jon Snow hair!"

"Right?"

"Caroline, he's really hot. Are you sure there's noth—"

"Who's really hot? Can I see?" Hannah's younger sister, Michaela, appears in the corner of the frame, near their bedroom door. Hannah shrieks and shoots out of her chair to slam the door, shouting that Michaela will regret life if she doesn't stay out. I can't help laughing. The sisters share the room, and Michaela—three years younger than us—has always wanted to be a part of whatever we're doing. It drives Hannah crazy.

"I miss that so much," I say when she returns to her desk.

"You can have her. I'll Bubble Wrap her, pack her in a box, and send her to you. Speaking of which . . . it's box time. You first."

Sitting on my nightstand is a box wrapped with a brown grocery bag, my address and Hannah's return address written in black marker. We sent each other care packages, promising to wait to open them until we could do it together. Now I pull the box onto my lap and start peeling away the paper.

"Since I've been working so many hours, there's a common theme to this one," she says. "I hope it doesn't suck."

Inside is a four-piece box of chocolate saltwater taffy, a plush Woodstock, a small woodcarving of my name, and a tiny bottle of sand tied with a bit of twine—all things from Cedar Point.

"It definitely doesn't suck." I unwrap a piece of taffy and pop it in my mouth. The taste recalls memories of the amusement park. Hannah's dad works in the maintenance department so we grew up at Cedar Point. As little girls we had favorite horses on the carousel—we called them ours and pretended to grant other park guests permission to ride them—and as we got older, we turned into bona fide coaster enthusiasts. One evening last spring, when the park wasn't crowded, we rode the Blue Streak fifteen times in a row. "Now that I'm completely homesick, it's your turn."

Hannah tears into her box and pulls out one of the scarves I bought at the Friday Market. It is blue, orange, and red with a bit of orange fringe. I also added a brass Sphinx that I had

Tarek buy for me (since I was still afraid to haggle on my own) and a bottle of Egyptian sand.

"This is so beautiful." Hannah drapes the scarf around her shoulders. "Maybe I could ship myself to you instead of sending my sister."

"I wish you could."

"Me too."

"I should go." The dawn *adhan* will be starting soon. Even though I slept a few hours before our chat, it's still the middle of the night and I'm tired. "Give my love to everyone."

"Just so you know," Hannah says, "Owen is not dating Jessie. She likes him, but he only went to Emilee's party with her because he was too nice to say no."

One ill-advised text message aside, Owen and I have upheld our agreement. No e-mails. No phone calls. He didn't even respond to that text. "It's not my business anymore."

"Are you over him?" Hannah asks. "Because I don't think he's over you."

"I'm trying to be. He needs to do the same."

"That's what I told him."

"I'll send you another box soon," I say, thinking that when Mr. Elhadad is feeling better, I'll ask him to drive me to Khan el-Khalili so I can find something really special for Hannah. "Love you to the moon."

"And back."

We log off and I sit in the darkness, listening to the incessant hum of traffic and the near-constant honking that has become the background music of my life. When the *adhan* begins, I open the doors and drag my chair onto the balcony to listen. It isn't so scary anymore, especially now that I'm getting used to it, now that I know people who rise before the sun to say the prayers and perform the movements that accompany them.

My thoughts wander to Adam, and I wonder if he ever grumbles about having to wake so early in the morning and how often he goes back to sleep afterward. Hannah was correct that I didn't share the whole story. Adam and I are in a gray zone between strangers and friends, but somehow that doesn't stop me from thinking about him more often than I should. And it doesn't stop my heart from thumping like a dryer full of sneakers.

After the last strains of the call to prayer fade, I climb into bed and tip into sleep almost immediately.

I wake when my cell phone beeps with an incoming text.

From Adam.

The sun is barely up and my phone says I've been asleep for only about five hours. It's odd that he would text me at all, but even more odd that he would send it so early in the morning.

But the oddest thing of all is that he sent the message in the hours after I'd been thinking about him, which means he must have been thinking about me, too.

My father must take a rest from driving for the next two weeks. If you need to go somewhere, please tell me and I will drive you.

What about the restaurant? I text back.

He needs his business more than I need my job and now we have hospital debt to repay.

Will you be able to go back?

There are too many people looking for work.

I stop myself from asking how long it will take to pay off Mr. Elhadad's medical bills. This is not a boundary I have any business crossing and I don't want to make Adam feel worse about sacrificing his job. Could it take his family years to pay down the debt? What if they can never pay it back? My heart breaks for Adam, for the dreams he has to put on hold.

I need a driver today. My thumbs fly across the keypad as I decide to keep Adam as busy as possible. My savings—mostly money earned babysitting the Wagner twins down the street—are not bottomless, but I will give all of it to him if necessary.

Destination?

Anywhere. You choose.

CHAPTER 14

*T*he place Adam chooses is an old, walled-off portion of the city where a heavy wooden door is set into an ornately carved stone gatehouse. A blue plaque affixed to the wall reads SHARIA MARI GERGES, but that is only the name of the road, not the landmark. Although there are small clusters of tourists here and there, it is quiet and not crowded with people.

Adam holds open the door for me. I sneak a glance up at his face as I pass and find him watching me with those light brown eyes. Curious eyes. He offers a shy smile and I'm not sure what's happening, but I think I like it. I smile back. Look away first.

We pass through the gatehouse into a long, narrow court-yard where cacti and palms rise up from garden beds that run down the middle. At the opposite end of the courtyard, a stone staircase leads up to a double-spired church with a cross atop each spire.

"What exactly is this place?"

"The Coptic section of the city is where the oldest Christian churches stand," Adam says. "And just beyond the walls you will find the oldest synagogue in Cairo."

"I didn't realize—I mean, I'm kind of embarrassed to admit that I didn't think other religions were allowed here."

"I will not try to tell you that Christians and Muslims always worship peacefully in Egypt," he says, "because Christians were killed a few months ago in a bombing of the Coptic cathedral. But Egypt has a small Christian population and this place holds some of their history. Maybe your history too?"

Adam could have taken me to a famous mosque or even to a modern Egyptian shopping mall—either of those things would have been perfectly fine—but to bring me to a place of Christian history strikes me as a deliberate choice. A really thoughtful choice. "Thank you."

"I confess that I have never been here," he says. "So everything I am telling you is only what I have learned on the Internet this morning."

"That's still more than I know."

"So this church is *Sitt Mariam*, which means St. Mary,

but it is more commonly called al-Muallaqah—the Hanging Church—because it was built on top of an ancient Roman fortress. Inside I think we will see how it is possible to build a church without no foundation."

The courtyard walls are adorned with brightly colored mosaics of Jesus, Mary, Joseph, angels, and either saints or holy men—even I'm not completely sure—their halos set in golden tiles that sparkle in the sun. One mosaic depicts Joseph leading a donkey carrying Mary and the infant Jesus on its back. I know this image. "This is the holy family's flight to Egypt."

When I made my first communion, Grandma Rose gifted me with a thick book filled with Bible stories that I would sometimes read at night before bed. One of the most exciting and scary stories was about how King Herod ordered all the firstborn sons of Judea to be killed because he feared Jesus would one day take his throne, so Joseph took the family and escaped to Egypt. In the story, angels appeared to him in a dream when it was safe to go home.

"None of the Bible stories ever describe what their everyday lives might have been like. They focus on Jesus as an adult, performing miracles and dying on the cross," I explain as we make our way up the stairs to the church. "So it's a little surreal to think about his family living here, just being regular people."

Grandma Irene has a picture of Jesus hanging on the wall of her living room. He has white skin and blue eyes, and Dad always calls him Classic Rock Jesus. Never have I believed Jesus was white—geography and history say otherwise—but being here in Egypt makes it that much easier to imagine. The holy family would probably have looked like the people around me; they would have had brown skin like Adam.

"They traveled through the country for more than three years," he says. "And it is believed that while in Cairo they lived on the site of what is now the crypt beneath the Abu Serga church. We can see the site if you like."

"I would."

Even though my brain has wrapped itself around the fact that Christianity has roots in this part of the world, it doesn't stop me from expecting the Hanging Church to look like our church back home. Ours is also called St. Mary's, but it is a Gothic-style Roman Catholic church nearly the size of a cathedral, with soaring arches and big stained-glass windows. So I'm stopped in my tracks when I see that this church is covered in the arabesque patterns of Egypt. Painted designs tangle themselves around the arches between the pillars. Carved wooden patterns cover the walls. Even the woodwork of the pews is an intricate lattice so different from the plain benches at home. But as I stand in the main aisle, the smell of polished wood and candle wax and the faint scent of incense are *exactly* the same.

"This is really beautiful."

"It is," Adam agrees. "The seating is strange to me. At the masjid we have only a large empty space for worship."

"Honestly, I'm not really sure how Masses work in this church because I don't think Coptic Orthodox and Roman Catholic are the same," I say. "But we sit for Scripture readings and for the homily, and stand and kneel for everything else."

"Now I must admit I thought all Christians believed the same things."

"There are more kinds of Christians than I could possibly name," I say. "And I don't really know what makes them all different, other than they disagree on parts of the theology."

"It is the same with Islam."

"Really?"

"Sunnis and Shiites have different ways of believing and there are other smaller sects," Adam says. "But all Muslims worship the same God."

"Same with Christians."

We stand in silence for a moment and I'm not sure if we've bridged a gap or made it wider.

"So I have an idea." Adam beckons me to follow him to where a small tour group is gathered around a Plexiglas panel in the floor. We stand close enough to hear their guide explain that each end of the church is supported by a tower from an older Roman fortress, and that it's about eighteen meters to the original ground level.

"The roof," the guide says, "is made of wood because the weight of a stone roof would have collapsed the church."

We wait until the group moves on, then look down through the clear panel. I have never been very good with meters-to-feet conversions, but the ground is an uncomfortably long way down. After fifteen hundred years, I'm not sure why the church isn't sagging in the middle, but it's pretty amazing it's survived for so long.

From the Hanging Church we go see the crypt, visit a well said to be where the holy family drank, and stop to take pictures of the remains of the Roman fortress. There are a bunch of churches in the area, but Adam and I agree that two is enough for one day. Instead we wander the narrow alleyways, where vendors have tables filled with religious trinkets and replica icons like the ones inside the Hanging Church. I buy Virgin Mary icons for Hannah's mom and both my grandmas, as well as a crucifix for Mom. We don't have one in the apartment yet.

"So, um . . ." I don't want to assume Adam cleared his whole day for me, but I'm not ready for it to be over, either.

I like spending time with him. Like listening to his accent. And I really like looking at his face. "Is there anything else—?"

"Would you—?" Adam says at the same time. We both stop and he clears his throat. "Perhaps you would like to try a coffee or tea before we go?"

"I would. Yes."

Down one of the labyrinthine alleys we find a tiny coffeehouse with a couple of tables outside and an all-Arabic menu. Adam calls it an *ahwa* and explains that coffeehouses are popular places to hang out in Egypt.

"Sometimes on Sunday mornings, if I am not working, I will meet my friends to play football," he says. "Then we go to our favorite *ahwa* for coffee, maybe a little *shisha*, and watch English football on TV."

"Playing soccer would be so great," I say. "I haven't played since I left home."

"My team is only for men."

Our silence is not the comfortable kind as we claim an empty table. The boundary between us seems mutable. Sometimes it feels as if Adam and I are becoming friends, but other times a wall slams down between us, reminding me that his culture has so many strange-to-me rules. Finally I say, "I wasn't asking to be invited."

"I misunderstood," he says. "I'm sorry."

Desperately wishing we could hit the reset button on this whole conversation, I switch topics. "So, um—coffee?"

"You can choose no sugar, light sugar, or heavy," Adam says as a waiter comes out to take our order. "Egyptian coffee is bitter with no sugar, so I don't recommend it."

"What would you recommend for someone who doesn't drink coffee?"

He pauses for a beat, as if the idea is incomprehensible. Then, "Will you trust me to order something for you?"

"Yes, of course."

I listen as Adam speaks, trying to recognize familiar words, but Arabic is so fast and so different from English. Picking up the language is going to take baby steps.

"My mom wants me to learn a little Arabic," I say after the waiter leaves. "Aside from counting, I really don't know where to start."

"The first lesson is this," Adam says. "Muslims greet one another with *as-salāmu alaykum*, wishing God's peace upon the other person. There is endless disagreement over whether non-Muslims should be included in this greeting, so there may be fundamentalists who will not respond to you if you say it. But most people will, if your salaam is said with sincerity."

"*As-salāmu alaykum.*"

"Yes. Good. And then I would reply *wa'alaykum alsalam*, or—if I were of the opinion that I should not be offering God's peace to a Christian but did not want to be rude—I would simply say *wa'alaykum*, which means 'the same to you.'"

"Sounds complicated. Maybe it would be easier to just say hello."

He does the nod-shrug, which seems to be a trademark move for him. "Maybe. In that case you would say *marhaban*, which is more formal, or *ahlan wa sahlan*. The most common is simply *ahlan*."

I laugh. "Arabic is not going to be easy, is it?"

"English is also not easy."

"You speak very well."

"My father believes that understanding English is important," Adam says. "Most Egyptian schools do not have strong English-language programs, so he taught us himself. I practice more than my mother and sister."

The waiter returns, carrying two short glasses—one filled with coffee, the other with ice and a red-colored liquid. A lime wedge hangs on the rim of the second glass.

"*Karkadeh* is my sister's favorite," Adam says as the waiter places the red drink in front of me. "It is tea made from boiling the hibiscus. Because the day is hot, I thought you might prefer it to be cold."

I take a sip. The *karkadeh* is slightly tart—a little like cranberry juice—and sugary. "This is perfect. *Shokran.*"

Adam smiles. *"Afwan."*

"I have a question not related to language."

"Okay."

"How hard is it to wake up for the dawn prayer?"

He leans back in his chair and the sun glints off his curls as he shakes his head. *"Fajr* is so difficult for me. I set two alarms and still my mother must help me wake."

"Do you ever go back to sleep?"

"If I must work early—" He stops abruptly and looks a little stricken, as if it's just hit him again that he's sacrificed his dream. "Well, now perhaps I can go back to sleep."

"I don't think so. Tomorrow I need a driver."

"Caroline—" His eyes meet mine and I trap my hands between my knees to keep from reaching across the table, to keep from touching him. "This is not necessary. Already my family cannot repay the kindness your family has shown to us."

"Kindness isn't a debt."

"But—"

"Should we hire a new driver?"

He shakes his head, his cheek dimpling as he fights back a smile. "No one's skills would compare to mine."

"Well, you're not wrong about that," I say, and my own mouth curves in response to his laughter. "So where will you be taking me tomorrow?"

CHAPTER 15

Mom is at the clinic and I've already been down to the bakery for bread when Adam arrives for our next outing. He is wearing dark jeans and a blue button-up shirt with the sleeves rolled. The color looks so good against the warm brown of his skin that the urge to tell him so creeps into my mouth. Instead I say, *"Ahlan."*

He opens the car door for me, giving a little bow as he motions me in. *"Masā' al- khair."*

"What does that mean?"

Adam goes to the other side of the car, answering only after he is behind the steering wheel. "It means good afternoon and good evening."

"So fancy." I smile at him in the rearview mirror. "Just like your shirt."

"I wore it because we have a new customer." He pulls away from the curb and a horn blares behind us. I bite my lip to keep from laughing. "I will be providing airport service two times a week for an American expatriate, but it will not interfere with our arrangement."

"Excellent news. Hopefully you'll get back to cooking sooner rather than later."

He nods. "Inshallah."

I decide not to ask where we are going today, to just let myself be surprised by whatever he has planned. Even though visiting churches wasn't the most exciting thing to do, yesterday turned out to be just right.

"Can I ask you something?"

"Yes, of course."

"You play soccer with your friends and hang out at the *ahwa*, but what do girls do for fun?"

"My sister and her friends go to movies and listen to music. Some take ballet lessons or play sports. Aya redesigns the styles she sees in fashion magazines to make them halal—"

"Halal?"

"The opposite of haram," Adam explains. "In this case, my sister makes the clothes more modest, and then our mother sews them for her." In the rearview mirror I watch the corner of his mouth tilt up in a grin and he glances up at

119

me. "We also have football teams for women."

I grin back. "It's probably good that women don't play against men. It would be painful for the men when they lose."

His laugh is clear and strong. "I think you may be right."

Yesterday's misunderstanding behind us, I sit back and watch Cairo fly past the window. The sky is hazy with smog and the city looks kind of gray, despite the sun hanging full and bright in the sky. Mom and I have learned that leaving the balcony doors open invites the heavy, polluted air inside, so we open them only early in the morning or well after dark. The rest of the time we keep the air conditioner running. Balconies all over Cairo are hung with drying laundry and it makes me wonder if pollution affects the clothes.

"From here we must walk," Adam says as he squeezes the sedan into a space that doesn't seem big enough. When we get out, the front bumper is touching the back bumper of the car just ahead.

"In the United States you would not be allowed to park like that," I say. "In fact, I'm pretty sure no one would give you a license."

His cheek dimples as he fails to keep from smiling. "I'm telling you that I am a good driver. Did I not fit the car in the space?"

"You are terrifying."

"I am terrifying *and* good."

I laugh. "I like you."

The words slip out before I can stop them and the city around us slows to a crawl. Or at least that's how it feels. Embarrassment in agonizing slow motion.

"I mean—I just—I didn't mean I *like you* like you." The words stumble from my mouth, making the awkward silence between us even worse. "I'll just shut up now."

We walk many steps, about half a block, before Adam clears his throat. When he speaks, he doesn't really sound all that pleased. "I like you, too."

Part of me wants to do a cartwheel on the dirty Cairo sidewalk—the same part of me that wants to smile (at him) until my cheeks hurt—but I also understand that Adam Elhadad and I liking each other isn't really supposed to be a thing. Not a friend thing. Definitely not a more-than-a-friend thing. In this moment, the whole idea of wanting to keep men and women apart . . . kind of makes sense. The more time I spend with Adam, the more time I *want* to spend with him.

"I have been trying to be professional." He shakes his head. "I have not been trying very hard."

"It's my fault. I keep making you take me places."

"That is my job."

"You're *really* good at picking places."

"But don't you see . . . when I am choosing for you, I am thinking of you," Adam says. "And I should not be doing that."

"Do you want to take me home?"

His curls bobble as he shakes his head more vigorously. "No."

"Then let's not think about it," I say. "Let's just have fun."

Khan el-Khalili is everything I'd hoped it would be. Crazy. Crowded. Beautiful. Vegetable stalls stand next to silver jewelers, souvenir shops beside rug dealers, spice vendors alongside dress stores. The merchandise spills outside the spaces, into the narrow streets, into a riot of color—a living postcard.

There are more tourists than at al-Gomaa. More women, too. As Adam and I walk the winding alleys, men call out from the shops, trying to grab our attention. Men from the restaurants push paper menus in our faces. Every single one of them claims that what he has on offer is the best. Best food. Best prices. When I look too long at a table piled with little plush camels, the shop guy walks backward in front of me.

"For you I give best price," he says, holding a camel out in front of me.

"No, thank you."

"Only fifty pounds."

Adam laughs and speaks to the man in Arabic. The only thing I can pick out is something that sounds like *mish mish*.

"Twenty-five," the shopkeeper replies.

"Would you like to buy the camel for twenty-five pounds?" Adam asks me. "I think that is around three dollars."

As I hand the man three dollars, it strikes me that even fifty Egyptian pounds—around six US dollars—isn't very expensive. Is getting the best deal really so important? Especially when I have way more than six dollars in my wallet?

"So why are the vendors so pushy?" I ask Adam as we continue down the alley. "Are they desperate for sales or is that just the way it works here?"

"Both," he says. "Tourism is Egypt's largest business, but the revolution, the Russian plane crash in the Sinai, and bombings by the Islamic State all over the world have frightened some of the foreign visitors away. Many Egyptians are poor and must take every opportunity we have."

Since most of the factories in my hometown closed down or moved abroad, our local economy has relied heavily on tourism. If we lost the amusement park, the hotels and restaurants would lose many of the tourists. The desk clerks and housekeepers, waiters and bartenders, would be out of work. The economy would probably collapse. It's unlikely to happen, though, and I know it can't really compare to Egypt—we don't have children begging in the streets—but I get the gist of what Adam is saying. No one should have to hustle so hard to make such a small amount of money.

"What did you say that made him drop his price?" I say. "Something *mish mish*?"

"I said *fil-mishmish*, which means that will never happen," Adam says. "Never will I pay so much for this thing."

"Fil-mishmish," I repeat softly to myself.

"Very good," he says. "Also, I reminded him that his wares are made in China. Perhaps six dollars is not so much money, but the camel is worth much closer to three."

"Doesn't paying more help him?"

"Yes, but haggling is also the Egyptian way."

We stop at a store that sells only silver jewelry—necklaces, bracelets, rings, earrings—where I haggle with the English-speaking shopkeeper over a cuff bracelet covered in hieroglyphs for Hannah. Adam grumbles that I paid too much.

"I thought the price was fair."

"You are like your father," he says.

I bump my elbow against his as we walk. "Apparently you are like yours, too."

At a perfume shop, I let the shop man convince me to try a bit of lotus oil. He rubs it on the inside of my wrist and I bring it to my nose. The scent is lush and sweet and almost tropical, and if Hannah were here, I would turn to her for a second opinion. Even Owen would be able to tell me if the scent was right for me.

As I bring my nose to my wrist a second time, I look at Adam. His eyes—already watching me—go wide, as if my wrist would be his undoing. He gives a quick shake of his head and develops a very sudden, very intense interest in a hookah pipe. I sniff my wrist again. Maybe he's wise to play it safe. The scent is definitely tempting.

The evening call to prayer begins as I pay for the oil. Outside, some of the shopkeepers hang signs in the window that say CLOSED FOR 10 MINUTES TO PRAY. The sun hangs low in the sky and it will soon be dark.

"Don't you need to pray?"

"The true answer is yes," Adam says. "But I do not want to leave you alone in the souk. So I will try to make it up later."

"You can do that?"

"It is not the best." He motions toward all the people around us, still going about their day. "But this is also life in Egypt."

My phone beeps with an incoming text from my mom. **About to close up. Should we try going out for dinner tonight?**

I'm at Khan el-Khalili. Come here?

How will I find you?

"Where can we meet my mom if she joins us?" I ask Adam. "Maybe at a restaurant?"

He names a place in the middle of the souk and I text Mom, telling her we will wait for her there.

"I'm sorry if this ruins your plans for the day," I say.

"Nothing is ruined," he says. "I was going to suggest a *taameya* cart, so if you would like to have dinner with your mother, I can return when you are ready to go home."

"Will you join us?"

"I should not."

"Adam, it doesn't make sense for you to hang around by yourself until we're finished," I say. "And you need to eat too. Please stay."

He hesitates and there's a struggle between his eyebrows over whether he should be Friend Adam or Driver Adam. Finally he says, "For you, I will stay."

"Thank you."

"So before your mother texted, my plan was for you to try *taameya* and then perhaps go see the *tanoura* dance at Wekalet El Ghouri," Adam says. "Perhaps she would like to see it too."

"I don't know what that even means, but if it's an Egyptian thing she probably would."

The lights come up in the shops as Adam and I walk to the restaurant, casting a carnival-like atmosphere over the Khan. I can't help thinking that walking through the souk, sharing a meal (even street food), and going to a show seems a lot like . . . a date.

CHAPTER 16

We take our time walking through the Khan, pausing at a shop that offers belly-dancing costumes in every color imaginable. The skimpy outfits seem incongruous in a country where women don't show much skin, but Adam explains that modern belly dancing has evolved from a form of folk dancing that women did in the presence of other women.

"There are dancers who are held in high regard and tourists pay to see them dance on the Nile dinner cruises," he says. "And there have been belly-dance competitions on the television, but many Muslims believe the dance is haram and that the dancers are no better than prostitutes."

"What do you think?"

He shrugs. "Some men find it sexy, but I do not think about it at all."

I toy with the idea of buying a belly-dance costume for Hannah, then laugh to myself as I imagine how outraged her mother would be. Not so different from the Muslims who think it's haram.

By the time we reach the restaurant, Mom is standing beside the front door. I give her a hug. "How was your day?"

"A very sweet old lady tried to give me a goat as thanks for a pair of bifocals."

"A *goat*? You said yes, right?"

Mom laughs. "This was not a cute little thing like you see on YouTube, Caroline. He was big and beardy and I'm pretty sure he wanted to trample me to death."

"Sigh."

Saying the word—instead of actually sighing—is a goofy Hannah-and-me thing, but it makes my mom laugh again. She bumps her shoulder against mine. "If you want to get a pet, you can, but maybe think smaller. Like a goldfish or a bird."

I remember the birds that Adam and I saw at the Friday Market.

"I can drive you," he says, and I smile at the way he read my mind.

"Yeah, maybe. Since I can't have a goat."

Mom just shakes her head, smiling as she links her arm through mine, and says, "Let's go eat."

The restaurant calls to mind the Hanging Church, with ornate wooden carvings on the walls and an arched ceiling painted with arabesque designs. We are seated at a brass-topped table with two wooden chairs and a tiny burgundy velvet couch that I claimed for myself. Adam excuses himself to wash his hands.

"So I asked OneVision to hire a male doctor for the clinic," Mom says. "And he started today. His name is Jamie and he only just finished his residency—he's *so* young—but I think our patients are going to like him."

"That's great," I say. "Now maybe the old man with the cataracts will come back."

"I hope so."

Adam returns and Mom asks him to order for us.

"Choose your favorites," she says. "Or better yet, what you would make if you had the chance."

The way his eyebrows creep close together as he studies the menu makes me feel bubbly inside. His seriousness is adorable, but I know that as a cook this decision is probably important to him. If Mom wasn't with us, I'd just sit and stare at him. Instead I show her my market purchases and tell her how I am slowly getting the hang of haggling.

"Very slowly," Adam says, not looking up from the menu.

"Hush, you." I reach across the table and give his shoulder a playful shove. "I did *okay*."

The waiter arrives and Adam speaks to him in Arabic, then translates. "I have ordered *shai*—hot tea with sugar and mint— and, to start, a meze plate with hummus, baba ghanoush, *feteer meshaltet*, *gebna makleyah*, *warak enab*, and *taameya*."

"I know hummus and baba ghanoush," Mom says. "But you lost me with the rest."

"*Feteer* is a layered pastry that is sweet or savory," he says. "This one will have cheese, olives, and red peppers as the filling. *Gebna makleyah* is cheese that has been fried. *Warak enab* is grape leaves stuffed with rice and beef—"

"Oh, I know this one," she says. "We just call it stuffed grape leaves."

Adam nods. "You may know *taameya* as falafel, but in Egypt we use also fava beans instead of hummus."

"All of this sounds wonderful," she says.

"My favorite to eat is *gebna*, but my favorite to prepare is *feteer* because there is no end to the combination of ingredients for the filling."

"Do you cook at home a lot?"

"When everyone in my family is working or at school, my *teta*—my grandmother—does the cooking. She lives in the apartment next to ours, and, like me, she loves to cook," he says. "But when I have free time, I try to prepare dishes from other countries of the world. The last time I made jerk chicken from Jamaica."

131

"Jerk chicken is one of Casey's favorites," Mom says. "We went to Jamaica for our honeymoon and I swear he ate it every day."

"Have you been to many countries?" Adam asks.

"Just Jamaica and Germany—some of my ancestors were German—but we've traveled all over the United States. When Caroline was a little girl, we drove from Ohio to San Francisco, California, stopping at the national parks and monuments."

The waiter brings a glass teapot with a red spout and gold lotus flowers painted around the belly, and pours the tea into matching glasses.

"I would like to visit America one day," Adam says. "But I don't know if it is possible. It costs a lot of money to travel and I have heard that Muslims are unwelcome."

"That's not exactly true," Mom tells him. "There are some Americans who equate Islam with terrorism, but—"

"They are ignorant, then," he says, cutting her off. "If they knew the truth of Islam, they would understand that those who kill in the name of Allah are not truly Muslim. They bend the scripture to fit their twisted deeds."

"I know," she says. "But it's difficult to convince Americans when they are inundated with TV news about ISIS attacks. And when trying to figure out all the players in the political game gets too complicated, they throw up their hands and blame all Muslims."

"This is unfair."

"As unfair as being a woman out walking in Cairo," I point out.

"It is not the same." Adam slaps his palm against the table, rattling the glasses, startling me. I'm not afraid of his outburst, but it makes me realize he is still mostly a stranger. He blows out a breath to calm himself as he rakes his fingers through his curls. "I am sorry, Caroline, but none of those men on the street believe you secretly wish to murder them. And our politicians do not appear on television saying how they wish to keep you out of Egypt because you worship in a different way."

I look into my tea glass, stung by his rebuke—and the truth in his words. Mom is quiet too, and a thread of awkwardness zigzags around the table, connecting all three of us. I glance at Mom, glance at Adam, but none of our gazes quite meet. We're all embarrassed, and it seems like none of us knows how to lead the conversation back to a comfortable place.

Finally, the waiter arrives with a big circular plate filled with all the things Adam ordered, as well as a smaller plate piled with bread, and I feel a rush of relief. Adam smiles and explains to Mom, as he had with me, that it is customary to use your right hand for eating. "It is especially so when you are all dipping from the same bowl," he says. "Also, it is okay for you to eat with your fingers."

We sample all of the foods on the meze plate as Adam tells us the ingredients of each dish. When we try the *warak enab*, he shares a story about how his grandmother taught him to roll the grape leaves when he was little.

"I have an older cousin who would tease me," he says. "Asking why do I want to learn to do women's work. But Teta told me that many of the finest chefs are men, so I did not let my cousin bother me too much."

Mom drags a bit of bread through the last of the baba ghanoush. "I think my favorite is the *taameya*."

"Mine is the *gebna*," I say, hoping Adam doesn't think I chose it just because it's his favorite. *Gebna* reminds me of *saganaki*, the flaming cheese we order from our favorite Greek restaurant back home. "Fried cheese is never a bad choice."

Our gazes meet and he smiles. "Exactly this."

The food is barely gone when the waiter whisks away the empty plates and brings another platter, this time heaped with different kinds of kebab. As we eat *kofta* and lamb and chicken, I envy how much easier it is for Adam to talk to my mother than to me. She is the adult—almost like a chaperone—and her presence puts him at ease.

Following dinner, we walk from the Khan to Wekalet El Ghouri, an arts center inside a sixteenth-century stone complex that also houses a mosque, a Muslim school, and a *khanqah*, which Adam explains is a place where the Sufi brotherhood once met. "Tonight there is a show, a *tanoura* dance," he tells Mom. "If you would like to see it."

She buys tickets with neither of us knowing what to expect.

The music begins first, mostly drums and a wooden instrument that makes me think of the recorders my class learned to play in elementary school. It has a wider bell at the bottom, and when I ask Adam what it's called, he says it is a *mizmar*. Then the performers—whirling dervishes—come out, wearing white turbans and costumes with wide, full skirts decorated in a rainbow of colors. They start to dance, spinning in a way that makes the skirts flare out into circles. Round and round they whirl—how they don't get dizzy and fall down is a mystery—song after song. Sometimes they carry props that look like bedazzled drums, and other times they hold large circles of fabric that match their skirts, spinning the circles over their heads as they whirl. I snap a few photos with my phone—the dervishes a blur—and clap along with the audience around us. My elbow bumps repeatedly against Adam's arm, and when I glance up, I catch him watching me.

The air around us feels electric as our eyes meet, and I can't stop myself from smiling at him. He tips his chin toward the performance, his eyes still met with mine. "You should watch the dance."

"I should," I say, forcing my attention back on the dervishes, but every time I sneak a peek at Adam (too often), he is looking at me.

It is late when we arrive at our apartment, the sun long gone. Mom insists that Adam drop us off at the building instead of accompanying us upstairs, but he still opens the car door for us.

"Those dancers were amazing." Mom twirls on the sidewalk and hands him a Casey Kelly–sized tip. "Thank you for inviting me, and for giving Caroline and me more than your fair share of time."

"The pleasure was mine." Adam touches his hand to his chest, over his heart, and glances at me. "Good night."

I'm following my mother to the elevator when my phone buzzes in my pocket.

Will you need a driver again soon?

Over my shoulder I see Adam leaning against the car, waiting for my reply. I smile to myself as I type the answer. **Yes.**

CHAPTER 17

I would like to show you something different," Adam says as I lock the front door behind me. Usually I meet him down on the street, at the car, but today he came upstairs. "But it is better to take the metro, which means we must walk to the station."

I've ridden the subway in New York with my parents, so I have no trouble with the idea of taking public transportation, but I am a little nervous about being packed in a train with a bunch of Egyptian men, a fear I share out loud.

"So the first two cars on the metro are only for women," he says as the elevator descends. "I will not allow anyone to harass you, but you may feel more comfortable riding in the women's car."

"Where are we going?"

"Tahrir Square," he says. "It is the place where the Egyptian revolution overthrew the government. In the time since, graffiti artists have made artwork on some of the buildings that is very good and I thought perhaps you might like to see it."

Sometimes, when we were bored, Owen and I drove out Old Railroad to the Miller Road viaduct, where decades of graffiti was layered on the abutment. Hearts. Stars. Words of insult. Words of love. And a lot of overlapping school colors. I took a picture every time we went and every picture was different from the last.

"Yeah, definitely."

"The thing you must know . . . do you remember last night how your mother said Americans cannot follow all the players in the political game?"

"Yes."

"Ever since the revolution, our government has changed, but the game has not," he says. "Wages have improved, but not enough that we do not struggle. We hoped our country would follow in the footsteps of Tunisia toward a more democratic government, but that has not happened."

We pause at an intersection for the traffic to pass, then dash across in a gap. A truck driver blares his horn at us.

"The criticism that began a revolution has become unwelcome," Adam continues. "Homes are raided and Egyptians have been detained by the police—some for years—accused of supporting the opposition. So what I am telling you is that while we are in the square, we must be careful of what we say."

"Is this—" I lower my voice. "Is this going to be dangerous?"

"I do not think so," he says. "People will know you are a foreigner by your hair, but we will attract attention by being together in public and using English. Speaking too loudly about the revolution might raise suspicion."

"So why go?"

"Cairo is my home and now it is yours," he says. "Should we not be free to go wherever we want?"

There isn't much comfort in the idea that we simply have a right to visit Tahrir Square, especially not if there's a chance Adam might be arrested. I don't want to be responsible for that. And I'm kind of scared. "Maybe—um, maybe we should go somewhere else."

"I would like you to see this."

Swallowing my hesitation, I nod. "Okay."

Crossing the El-Rawda bridge on foot is no different from walking through the airport, shopping at al-Gomaa, or trying to go to McDonald's—almost every man who passes feels the need to lay eyes on me. Some glance. Some blatantly stare. One runs a slow tongue across his lower lip. Having Adam with me makes me feel a little less helpless, but I can't imagine being an Egyptian woman trying to live a normal life. Do they get up in the morning and plan routes with the least amount of men? Do they wish themselves invisible? Because right now I wish I had that superpower.

Fifteen minutes later we reach the metro station.

As Adam teaches me how to buy a ticket from the auto-mated kiosk, a man comes up and says something to him in a sly voice. Adam keeps his eyes trained on the machine as he responds, but his tone is cold and hard. The other man laughs and offers a parting shot before he melts into the crowd.

"What did he say?"

"Telling you will only make you angry."

"Then I definitely need to know."

Adam sighs and for a moment I fear he's not going to tell me. His face colors when he says, "He called you my American whore. I told him . . . well, I told him what he could do to himself. And that is when he laughed and said I should save it for you."

"You were right." My hands tighten into fists and I want to charge into the station, find that guy, and punch him in the face. "And for a place that's supposed to be so conservative about sex and dating, these guys sure think about it a whole lot. Meanwhile, the foreign whore hasn't actually ever had sex."

"You should perhaps lower your voice."

"Why? Everyone else in Cairo seems perfectly comfortable talking about my sexual experience," I say. "Why shouldn't I?"

"It is just that—"

"No, I get it, Adam." I shove my ticket into the turnstile and snatch it out from the other side. "Be quiet. Be invisible unless some man wants to look at you."

"I was not going to say that," he protests. "I was just going to say that with time it will not bother you so much."

"Are you kidding me?" I say, whirling to face him. He winces, as if he's embarrassed to be having this conversation in public, which only fuels my anger. "Do you think your sister has actually gotten used to boys whispering obscene things in her ear? Or that I will ever be able to ignore someone calling me a whore? No woman should have to get over it."

His shoulders sag. "You are right."

The thing is, I don't know if he's agreeing because he actually believes it or if he just wants me to stop talking about this on a subway platform thick with people who might overhear—until he reaches out and takes my hand, deliberately touching me for the first time. Adam's palm is warm and a little rough as he guides me to a spot where a large clump of women wait for the train.

"This is where the women's cars will be when the train arrives," he says. "The third stop will be Sadat. Exit there and I will find you. Okay?"

"Sadat." I repeat the name of the stop, even though I don't want to get on the train without him, don't want to let go. A hot wind rushes down the platform, announcing the oncoming train. Adam gives my hand a reassuring squeeze, then disappears into the crowd. A middle-aged lady beside me clicks her tongue in disapproval, but an ancient, tiny woman—her brown face carved deep with wrinkles and her uncovered hair the color of a thundercloud—tucks her hand beneath my arm. The train doors slide open and she ushers me into the subway car.

She sits, but I grab hold of the overhead handrail, letting the older ladies—even the tongue clicker—and young mothers have the available seats. The old woman takes a worn copy of the Quran from her bag and reads as the car sways along the track. The air is warm and thick, perfume-sweet and sweaty, and it gets harder to breathe the more crowded the car becomes.

One stop.

Some of the women watch me with curious eyes. Even though my clothes are pretty conservative, my hair is an attention magnet. I consider buying myself a scarf to make me less conspicuous, but my hair is part of who I am and my skin is still white. So I don't know if that's the answer at all.

Two stops.

A man with a briefcase tries to barrel his way onto the car. A couple of the women block his entrance while others shout him out. None of it fazes the old lady, who continues reading the Quran.

Just before the third stop, she stows her holy book and extends a hand so I can help her to her feet. She gestures at the doors. "Sadat."

Together we step into a crowd swollen by the crossing of two Cairo subway lines. People push past us as we stand in the middle of the platform, but she holds my arm until Adam arrives. Before she releases me, I place my hand on top of hers and smile. *"Shokran."*

She gives me a gentle pat and smiles back, and then she is gone.

CHAPTER 18

*T*he graffiti around Tahrir Square (actually a circle) reminds me of the East Side Gallery in Berlin. My parents took an anniversary trip to Germany and Mom returned with a whole series of photos of the art that has been painted on a long segment of what was once the Berlin Wall. Tahrir feels more immediate and raw but bears a lot of the same themes. Portraits of the people killed during the January 25 revolution. Caricatures of Hosni Mubarak—the president deposed by the revolution—that depict him swinging from a noose. Che Guevara with a long beard and a Muslim prayer cap. There is even one of Barack Obama as the tap of a bloody shower, representing the United States' support for the Mubarak regime. I don't understand the revolution enough to grasp the role my own country played, but clearly some Egyptians think it was not a good one.

"The government tries to paint over these works, as if removing the images will remove our memories," Adam says. "But the artists keep returning."

I'm snapping a shot of Snow White toting a machine gun when a police officer approaches us. I slip my phone into my bag as he and Adam exchange words. Adam gestures toward me and I recognize a word that sounds like *American*. Finally he digs into the pocket of his jeans and hands over a couple of bills.

"What just happened?" I ask as the officer walks away.

"He pretended to believe I am your tour guide," Adam says. "And he said he could make our protection a priority, to keep others from thinking we are trying to incite protest. For a price, of course."

"And you just paid him like it's no big deal?"

"What would you have me do?"

I shake my head. "This place is so messed up."

"And America is perfect?"

"No, but it's not like *this*."

"Just remember, after your country witnessed a revolution in Egypt, we watched what happened in Ferguson," he says.

"That was one city."

Adam's eyebrows lift. "Was it?"

The backlash from Ferguson spread, prompting an entire movement to protect black Americans from police brutality, so no . . . it wasn't just one city. The corruption here in Egypt isn't better or worse than back home. It's just different. But the people's response to corruption in both countries seems universal. "The whole world's pretty messed up, isn't it?"

"Perhaps," Adam says, then offers me a smile that makes my toes curl. "But there is also kindness everywhere."

True to the police officer's well-funded word, no one hassles us as we walk along Mohammed Mahmoud Street, looking at the images on the wall surrounding the American University of Cairo. Adam translates the words scrawled with the images.

Down with Mubarak.

Be afraid of us, government.

Glory to the martyrs.

It is still January Revolution.

"Even though they knew it would be dangerous, my parents brought us to the square so my sister and I could witness history as it was being made. My mother painted Egyptian flags on our cheeks and we danced when the Mubarak regime fell," Adam says. "Then Morsi, the next president, was removed. Now our leaders seem to be more concerned with eliminating opposition than meeting the demands of the revolution, so I fear we are back where we began. Those who led the uprising are in jail or have fled the country, and I do not think the people can rise up again."

"I'm sorry."

"Me too."

We stop at a tiny bookshop squeezed between a restaurant and a pharmacy, where I buy a photo book of revolution graffiti, including some of the art that's already been whitewashed away. We sit in the bookshop's café, sipping coffee and *karkadeh*, and Adam asks me about Ohio.

"Well, we don't have nearly as much sand and it's very green," I say. "Lots of farms and forests, and my town is right on Lake Erie, which is one of the Great Lakes."

I search the Internet for pictures of downtown Sandusky and Adam's eyes widen. "The buildings are so small and the streets so clean. And no traffic."

"We do get some traffic in the summer when the tourists come to Cedar Point." I bring up pictures of the amusement park and explain that it holds world records for the roller coasters. I tell him how Sandusky was once a stop on the Underground Railroad and how it was also home to a prison for Confederate officers during the Civil War. After meeting Aya, I put more personal pictures on the new phone, so I show Adam my house, my friends, and Owen.

"He is my ex-boyfriend," I say. "We've known each other since we started school, but we dated for three years."

Adam sits back in his chair and toys with his coffee glass.

He doesn't look at me and I can feel him pulling away. "That is a long time."

"Yes, it is."

"And you loved him?"

"Yes."

"Were you going to be married?"

"No. And we will be going to different colleges next year, so we would probably have broken up anyway," I say. "My religion has a lot of the same rules as yours. Some people choose to follow them. Some don't. As I loudly mentioned at the train station, Owen and I followed the rules."

Silence sits between us and I pull my lower lip between my teeth, willing Adam to say something. Anything. What if the way I feel about him is all in my head? What if the reason I like him is because he's the only guy I know in Egypt?

"Do you love him still?" he asks.

I love the way Owen's smile always felt like sitting in the sun. I love how unapologetic he was about telling groan-worthy jokes. I love that he was a great listener. I love that he always respected my personal boundaries. He was the perfect first boyfriend. But he didn't break my heart. "He will always be my friend."

Leaving me no hints as to whether he is satisfied with my answer, Adam digs into his pocket and pulls out his phone. He taps a few icons and then hands me the device. On the screen is a picture of him posing with three other guys.

"Bahar is on the left. He studies medicine at Cairo University," he says. "This one with the beard is his brother, Omar, who works as a baggage handler at the airport. And Magdi, on the right, repairs computers at a shop not far from here."

Omar is the tallest with tight spiral curls and a scruffy beard. Bahar's hair is short on the sides, slicked back on top. His eyes are the same dark brown as Omar's and their brotherhood is obvious. Magdi is the shortest and the most handsome of the three, with hair that's close-cropped all over and a wide, happy smile.

"They look nice," I say, giving the phone back. "Are they?"

Adam laughs a little. "Most of the time." He tucks the phone into his pocket. "Bahar has ambition. He keeps a small book with his life goals, but the list has only things like finish university, get a job, find an apartment, get married. We say, 'Bahar, why can't you keep this in your head? Do you think you will forget to finish university without a list?'"

"What does he say?"

"That the list is a reminder that anything not on the list is not important."

"Who can argue with that?"

"Exactly," he says. "We call Omar *rad*"—Adam pronounces

it like "rod"—"because he is easily satisfied. He sometimes grumbles about politics and wages, but he enjoys his job and now his mother is beginning to talk of finding him a wife. He says okay to that, too."

"He just goes with the flow, huh?"

Adam cocks his head as he considers. "I like that. Yes. He goes with the flow."

"And Magdi?"

"He never has any money because he spends it on clothes and going out to clubs," he says. "He likes dancing, smoking *shisha*, playing football, and meeting girls. He is my best friend."

"Really? I would have guessed Bahar."

"My mother would be happy if that were true. She thinks Magdi is a troublemaker, but we have been friends the longest time."

"Can I meet him?"

Adam's eyebrows pull together and there's a little line of worry between them. Like maybe he's jealous. "Perhaps that is not a good idea."

"Why? He sounds like the friend least likely to freak out to see you with a girl."

"This is true." He runs his hand up through his curls and that same worried look passes across his face again. "But he can be very charming."

"I'm pretty sure I can resist his charms." I pause to gather a little courage. "And there's no way I could like him more than I like you."

Adam's worry softens, and when he smiles, the boundary between us shifts to a new place that's both scary and exciting. I have never been a girl who pursues boys—Owen clicked into my life like a puzzle piece—so I'm unsure how to proceed with Adam. I look at our empty glasses. "Should we go?"

I leave money on the table for the drinks and we step out into the hazy sunshine. If I were with Owen, we would hold hands, but I am with Adam, we are in Egypt, and what's happening between us is too fresh to test in the middle of downtown Cairo. Also, there are way too many eyes watching us.

"You should know that Magdi is a shameless flirt," he says as we take a side street to the next major road. "Whenever he comes to my home, he flatters my grandmother and makes her giggle."

The computer shop is a tiny storefront with refurbished laptops for sale in the window. We step inside, where a guy sits behind a worktable, his dark head bent over a motherboard. He looks up and I'm startled by how much more handsome he is than in the picture. Magdi's eyelashes are deep black and so thick it's almost like he's wearing eyeliner. Adam's worry makes more sense to me now. I doubt his best friend has any trouble meeting girls, because it almost hurts to look at him. He appraises me silently as he stands and comes out from behind the table, then grins at Adam. The two friends greet each other with a hug and exchange words in Arabic.

"What did he say?" I ask Adam.

Magdi grins. "I ask him if he brings this girl for me, but he says not every girl is for me."

Adam rubs the back of his neck—a boy-bashfulness tell that seems to be universal—as Magdi laughs, clearly pleased to be embarrassing his friend. "Adam tells me Caroline"—he pronounces it *care-ooh-leen*—"is lovely but he lies. You are much more beautiful."

"The only thing better than your eyesight is your gift of flattery," I say, and Magdi doubles over with laughter.

"Her, I like." He says this to a stone-faced Adam. "Too good for you. She should be with me."

"You have already too many."

Magdi winks at me. "I think perhaps you are for him."

My face is still warm as the afternoon call begins and he locks the door and puts up a sign like the ones in the Khan. CLOSED TEN MINUTES FOR PRAYER. Adam and Magdi excuse themselves to the back room, leaving me alone in the tiny showroom. I take a seat at Magdi's worktable, and through the doorway I see them as they take turns going into the bathroom to wash, then as they start their prayers. They stand, quietly reciting prayers. Bow. Kneel with their heads to the floor. Even though they are praying together and within my sight, it feels too intimate to watch. I look away and play a silent game on my phone, matching colored fruit as the two guys worship.

Magdi comes out first to reopen the store. "Adam has not yet finished. I think he says extra prayers so I will not steal you away."

"Fil-mišmiš," I say, which cracks him up all over again.

Magdi places a hand over his heart, trying not to laugh as he feigns sadness. "I am a broken man."

Adam emerges from the back room, the ends of his curls damp from washing his face. "We should leave the broken man to his work. If he loses his job, the shops at the mall will surely suffer."

"We will see you later?" Magdi asks Adam, eyebrows raised as if they've already discussed plans for the evening.

"Perhaps."

"Lovely Caroline," Magdi says, kissing the back of my hand. My stomach aches from all the laughing this guy has made me do. "When you are finished with Adam, you will find me waiting here."

CHAPTER 19

I sit in the front seat of the car for the very first time as Adam drives us to the next somewhere. Somewhere he claims I will like and I believe him because he hasn't been wrong yet. He drives with his left hand and rubs his right hand down his jeans-covered thigh. I want to reach over and hold his restless hand, but I don't because all of this is totally new to Adam, and I am not entirely comfortable being the "experienced" person in this relationship.

"So you talked with Magdi about me," I say. "What about Bahar?"

"Bahar reminded me that becoming a chef is my goal and that one day my family will expect me to marry a Muslim girl," Adam says. "He says at best you distract me and at worst you are a sin."

"That's pretty harsh."

"The imam at the masjid would say that the devil does not whisper things you do not wish to hear; he tells you a beautiful story that you want to believe."

"I'm not a devil," I say. "And I don't want to be the Western girl who lured the good Muslim boy into the woods. Do you think we should stop this before we even start?"

"No." He says it quickly and with a certainty that makes me smile.

"Okay, so what *do* you think?"

"Before you came to Cairo, I had very little interest in girls," he says. "So why now am I interested? Why do you turn my head?"

"Good questions."

"At first I think it was because it is impossible not to look at you when you shine like the sun," he says. "But then—"

"It was Liverpool, wasn't it?" I deflect with a joke because there is an intensity in his eyes that overwhelms me. Falling in love with Adam would be such a short, easy leap.

He laughs. "If you were a Chelsea fan, I would not have introduced you to *koshary*."

"If you were a Chelsea fan, I wouldn't have let you."

"This is what draws me to you," he says. "The things you say make me smile, and you try to understand my language and my culture, even when it frightens you and makes you angry. Since we have met I feel both happy and terrible all of the time."

"I . . . don't know what to say to that."

Adam reaches across the center console and laces his fingers through mine. His palm is a little damp and my heart melts into a puddle. "Never before have I been so confused about what is right or wrong," he says. "My faith says I should not be with you, but this happiness . . ."

I nod as he trails off. "I feel it too."

The afternoon sun moves toward the horizon as we drive through the city, beyond Manshiyat Nasr, and up into a low, dun-colored range of hills. Adam keeps hold of my hand and tells me how he used to let Aya play with his hair when they were little. "She would make tiny braids all over my head," he says. "And Geddo—my grandfather—would be angry, saying it was improper for my hair to be in a girl's style, even though Aya would take the braids out as soon as she finished the last one."

"My grandma Irene has old-fashioned ideas about gender roles, too," I say. "Once I was helping her buy Christmas gifts for my cousins. Henry—who was about five or six at the time—wanted a book about a princess who disguised herself in a black costume to help people in need, but Grandma wouldn't buy it because the character was a girl. She thinks boys should read books about boys."

Adam nods. "Geddo also did not approve of Aya playing football with me, but my parents encouraged us to play together when we were small. It has changed a little bit as we got older, but they still believe we should be treated equally."

"I feel like having a good relationship with your sister is probably more important than your grandfather's opinion."

Adam laughs. "Geddo would have not agreed, but my sister and I do not fight often because we were raised to be friends."

"Do you get along with your grandma?" I ask.

"Yes," he says. "She has taught me everything I know about cooking, even when my grandfather did not approve. I think my father has an open mind today because he did not want to be like his father."

I tell him about some of Grandma Irene's missteps when Uncle Mike eloped with a black woman he met in Grenada while on leave from the Marines. "The first time he brought his new wife home, Grandma expressed surprise that Aunt Delphine had graduated from college. I guess Grandma thought everyone in the Caribbean lived in tin shacks or something. She was trying to be nice, but Uncle Mike said he could see her fretting over whether the oil in Aunt Delphine's hair was going to rub off on her couch.

Grandma Irene tries to be better about that stuff now and she adores their kids, but that doesn't mean she's not still racist. She would panic if she knew about you."

"Because to her all Muslims are terrorists?"

"I love her because she is my blood, but sometimes she makes it hard to like her."

"Geddo was the same for me."

"I guess we're stuck with the family we get, huh?"

Near the top of the highest hill we come to a small city with a road running along the edge of a cliff. From this high up we can see all across Cairo, even the pyramids in the distance.

"So this is Mokattam." He pulls the car off the road. "And just down below is the City of the Dead."

"What does that mean? Like zombies?"

He laughs. "No, it is el-Arafa—the cemetery—but there are people who live there, making their homes in the tombs and the mausoleums."

"The people live *in* the mausoleums? With the dead bodies?"

"Some were forced out of the city by the rising costs," he says. "Some stay to be with their ancestors."

I shudder a little. Although I don't believe in ghosts, I'm not sure I would want to live among the dead.

"Muslim families are very close," Adam says as we get out of the car. "My grandmother lives in the next apartment, my father's sister and her family lives down the hall, and my mother's brother lives on a nearby street with his wife. Always someone is visiting and life is not too private. The best thing about the dead"—he makes a sweeping gesture toward el-Arafa—"is that they keep their opinions to themselves."

We sit together on the hood of the car, and Adam takes my hand once more. His thumb grazes the back of my hand, raising the tiny hairs on my arms. Our shoulders press together. Knees. Even our feet touch as they rest on the front bumper. We've come a long way from our first day at the park when we had an entire bench and a takeaway order of *koshary* between us.

The sun has dropped low in the western sky, painting the world gold as it sinks toward the pyramids. "This is—wow." I push a tear away with my fingers as I try to laugh off the embarrassment of crying. "This is so beautiful."

"Caroline." The way he says my name is different now too. Lower. Softer. With a husky note that makes me want to capture the sound with my mouth, to feel his lips on mine. He says my name again and I hear the question in it, the words he can't articulate. Except I need Adam to lead the way, even if it means we both stumble a little.

I turn my head to look at him, smile at him, and my heart is a balloon that could float away, carrying me along with it. "If you do it exactly the way you just said my name, there's no way to get it wrong."

His fingers are featherlight against my skin as he touches my cheek, and then his mouth is against mine, soft and warm. Just a brush, then gone. The word perfect takes shape in my mind but is erased and rewritten when his lips find mine again.

Our smiles are bashful as we separate, our gazes meeting and skittering away as we adjust to this next new thing. The sky around us has darkened and the sun has spread fire along the edge of the world. The minarets and skyscrapers are black silhouettes, and the windows of the night city are beginning to come alive. Adam kisses me again with lips more confident, and I let my fingers steal up into his curls. We both sigh at the same time and I smile against his mouth.

"Perhaps—" Adam clears his throat, making me think touching his hair was too much for him to handle. It might have been too much for *me* to handle. "Would you like to take a walk? There is a café just down the road."

"That would be nice."

He holds my hand as we walk, as if the rules don't apply in Mokattam. A few cars are parked off the pavement, and a street vendor has set up a couple of small tables with plastic chairs for people to drink tea as they watch the sunset. Everyone around us seems to be coupled up. "Adam Elhadad, did you bring me to a make-out spot?"

"Yes," he says, and I love that he doesn't even pretend it was accidental. "But my intention was only for you to see the sunset."

I'm not sure I believe him, but it doesn't really matter. "I'm glad we came."

"Me too."

The café must have been beautiful once, but now it feels like a shabby echo, with faded tile floors and peeling paint. The waiter, who leads us to a table on the terrace overlooking the sparkling city, looks tired. As if the café is taking him with it as it fades. Beer is on the menu, which surprises me. "This whole mountain is like a little pocket of scandal, isn't it?"

"My downfall." Adam's tone is serious, but a smile threatens the corners of his mouth.

"Ooh, have I ruined you?"

He shakes his head no, curls bobbling, as he gives into the smile. "A little bit."

The waiter returns, and as we order hummus and bottles of Pepsi, Magdi comes onto the terrace with a girl. Her hair is long and dark, uncovered, and she wears black leggings beneath her tunic-length top. As they approach our table, I see how gorgeous she is. A perfect match for Magdi.

I stand as Adam stands, not really knowing what to do or say in this situation. Adam greets Magdi with a kiss on each cheek, then offers a salaam to the girl, who responds in kind.

"*Ahlan*," I say to her, and she smiles as she returns the greeting.

We settle around the table and Magdi introduces me to Hasnah. "She is my girlfriend in secret."

Hasnah explains in flawless English that they met in a club. "His family would never approve of me because I'm not devout enough. They have planks in their eyes where Magdi is concerned—they see him as their good Muslim boy—so it's easier to keep our relationship private."

The waiter brings our food and drinks, and Magdi orders *shai* for himself and Hasnah. As we dip into the hummus, she tells me that she is working on a dual degree in political science and international human rights law at the American University in Cairo. "Everyone has an opinion on what Muslim women should or shouldn't do," she says. "But very few ask us what we want. We need a louder voice in the world. We need defenders."

"I am your defender." Magdi flexes his biceps and Hasnah gives his shoulder a playful push.

"This is what I love about Magdi," she says to me, then kisses his cheek in front of everyone. "He is good-looking, uncomplicated, and I like spending time with him. That's enough for now. We both know it's unlikely we'll have a future together, but we're not hurting anyone."

Adam pulls his lower lip between his teeth, as if he's holding back a differing viewpoint—a smart move given what she just said about Muslim women and opinions. Magdi and Hasnah make it seem so easy, but is having a secret relationship really such a good thing? Owen used to take me to his family's annual Fourth of July picnic. And he always came over on Christmas Day, after he opened presents at his house. I loved his family almost as much as I loved him. Then again, Hasnah has made it clear that she and Magdi are a temporary thing. I glance across the table at Adam, and even though I'll be in Egypt for months, the thought of having to leave him behind already makes my chest hurt.

"Are you ready to go?" he asks.

I pull out my phone to check the time and notice two missed texts from my mom. **Leaving the clinic,** the first one says. Then, **Where are you?**

I text her back quickly. **On my way.**

Adam is quiet as we head down the mountain, and I worry that he might regret kissing me.

"Are you okay?" I ask.

"Kissing you does not feel wrong, but I am not comfortable with keeping secrets."

"What is the alternative?"

The answer is in his silence. If his family is not okay with him dating, it really doesn't matter if I am white, American, or Catholic. Even under the guise of being my driver, he is pushing up against a belief system that has been a part of his life forever. Still, I feel relieved when he takes my hand, when we are connected again. And when we reach Manial, he parks between the streetlight pools so the car is dark as we say good night. His fingertips rest on the back of my neck, his thumb near my pulse point, and his lips are warm against mine.

"You're very good at this," I whisper, my fingers finding the door handle. I don't want to get out of the car, because I am afraid Adam will think too much about how I know he is a very good kisser. And that I'll think too much about him using this newfound skill on his someday wife. But I kiss him one more time, then open the door. "Sweet dreams."

Mom is making pancakes when I come into the apartment. "Where ya been?" she asks. "Want some?"

"Yes, please." I tell her how Adam and I went to Tahrir

Square, and show her the book of revolution graffiti. "We also went up to Mokattam to watch the sunset."

"Oh, really?" Her eyebrows climb toward her hairline and I feel like I've confessed to something illicit. I rummage through the silverware drawer for knives and forks so I don't have to look her in the eye.

"It's just a really great view of the whole city," I say, pulling up a photo of the sunset on my phone. "Amazing, right?"

"You and Adam have been spending a lot of time together."

I shrug. "He's my driver."

"I know, but—"

"You were the one who wanted me out of the house," I say. "Now I am and it's a problem?"

"It's not a problem. I appreciate that he's helped you get more comfortable navigating the city, but I worry you're growing too attached. This is temporary for Adam and I just think—well, it might be healthy for you to make some other friends."

There's no way to tell her that her concern is completely legit, that I've already blown past the "getting too" stage of my attachment to Adam Elhadad. "Um, sure. Since there's a horde of new people out there just waiting to befriend me."

"Don't be sassy," she warns. "You and Adam's sister got along well."

"Okay. Fine."

"Your dad will be home in a couple of days and we've been invited to have dinner with the Elhadads." Mom hands me a plate of pancakes and the finality of her tone says the book is closed on this subject. "You can make plans with Aya then."

CHAPTER 20

*M*asoud gives me the stink eye as I come out of the elevator the next day and I am glad he doesn't know enough English to tell me exactly what's on his mind. I can probably guess, though. Especially when I see Adam leaning against the car, waiting for me. Everything about him takes my breath away. There's nothing more I want to do right now than to kiss him, but the *bowab*'s glare is like a laser beam pointed at my back.

"*Sabah al-khair,*" I say instead.

I must have practiced the words fifty times last night before I said them correctly. Mom shot into my room like a rocket when she overheard, excited by my effort to learn Arabic, and offered me her computer program.

Adam's face lights up in a way that makes me want to learn every single word. "Good morning to *you*."

"What are we doing today?"

"So I want to talk to you about this," he says. "I have tried to keep the cost of our adventures low because you are always the one to pay, but today—"

"Nothing has to change, Adam. If I can afford it, let's do it."

"Today I would like to pay."

"I really don't mind."

"I would like to pay." His voice is softer the second time, but there is a firmness in it that wasn't there before and I take the hint. Clearly this is something he feels strongly about.

"Okay."

Adam smiles. "*Shokran.*"

He tells me as we drive that we are doing three things today, and our first stop is at a crowded riverfront café in Maadi where a Liverpool friendly match is showing on TV. Even more significant, though, is that while we are drinking *karkadeh* and watching the pregame commentary, Magdi and Hasnah show up. This time I am included in cheek kisses and Hasnah pulls her chair beside mine, as if we've known each other for more than a day.

"I'm not a huge football fan," she confesses. "But it's not much fun being the only girl in a gang of boys."

I'm about to point out that Magdi and Adam are hardly a gang when a couple of guys arrive, wearing track pants and soccer shoes and looking a little damp with sweat. I recognize them as Omar and Bahar, and Adam confirms it when he introduces us.

"As-salāmu alaykum," I say, hoping it's okay to greet them both at the same time.

Omar's reply is warm and hearty, but Bahar is more reserved, his voice low as he says, *"Wa'alaykum."* And then his attention is gone (kind of like Adam's on the first day we met) and I wonder if I should feel hurt by his response.

Adam's friends all order hookah pipes and before long we have an apple- and cherry-scented cloud hovering above our heads. It doesn't stink like cigarettes, but the fruity smoke is not really an appealing alternative.

"Want to try?" Hasnah offers me the hose to her pipe.

There doesn't seem to be a huge difference between *shisha* and cigarettes—aside from fancy flavors and a more complicated delivery system—but I've never had much interest in smoking anything. "No, but thanks."

She grins. "More for me."

Beneath the table, I feel Adam's pinkie finger hook around mine. I smile at him. "No smoking for you, either?"

"I do not enjoy it."

Watching the soccer game doesn't exactly lend itself to getting to know his friends, but it's kind of nice to be part of a group. We high-five each other when Liverpool scores, and during the halftime break, Magdi tells me a story about how he and Adam used to steal mangoes from a street vendor in their neighborhood until Adam's father caught them. "First he says he will chop off our hands as punishment."

"Really?" I turn to Adam. "That doesn't sound like your dad at all. He's so nice."

"He wanted only to frighten us."

"We cry and drop to our knees, begging him to spare us," Magdi adds.

"He paid the vendor for all the mangoes we had stolen but made us repay him," Adam says. "On my next birthday, Teta gave me a small sum of money and my father took it as payment of the debt."

There are tears in Magdi's eyes as he laughs and Adam goes on, "He kept record of the payments in a book like we were businessmen instead of small boys, but that was the last time I ever stole anything."

"What about Magdi?"

Adam's friend winks at me as Hasnah rolls her eyes. "I may yet steal you away from him," Magdi says.

Omar opens up during the second half of the game, asking—

through Adam since Omar speaks very little English—about my home and how it compares to living in Egypt. I pass my phone around the table so Adam's friends can see the pictures of Sandusky and Cedar Point. Adam explains that my town is small and that the population is only about twenty-five thousand people.

All of them laugh, as if the number is incomprehensible—probably because there are about twenty million people living in Cairo—and Adam translates for Omar, who says, "Twenty-five thousand is the population of our apartment building, and they all need to use the lift at the same time."

Despite laughing at his brother's joke, Bahar doesn't warm up to me at all. He spends most of the game with his eyes glued to the television, engaging only to speak in Arabic to Omar or Magdi. Bahar ignores Hasnah and ignores me, and I hear the shortness in his responses whenever Adam tries to say something to him. I feel guilty for causing bad blood between friends, and this is one gap I don't think I can bridge.

Disappointment radiates off Adam like heat, until the referee blows the final whistle on the game, ending both Adam's and Liverpool's misery. Bahar practically jumps out of his chair, as if he can't wait to escape, and throws a good-bye over his shoulder as he bolts for the door. Omar offers an apologetic smile, then follows his brother out of the café. I catch a glimpse of sadness in Adam's eyes as he watches them leave. He's subdued when he asks me if I am hungry.

"I could eat."

"Good. Because it is time for the next thing."

"We'll see you later," Hasnah says, then covers her mouth with her hand as if she's spoiled a secret. "*Maybe*. Maybe we'll see you later."

Leaving the others behind, Adam and I walk down the road to a small marina filled with feluccas—wooden sailboats with canvas-shaded decks and large, curved sails mounted on angled masts. Our captain is a dark-skinned man named Osama, who takes my hand to help me aboard the boat. Adam and I sprawl beside each other on soft, colorful cushions, and when the boat is away from the dock, he puts his arm around my shoulders and brushes his lips against my temple.

"What made you decide to introduce me to Omar and Bahar?" I ask.

"I thought perhaps if they knew you, they would understand why I want to be with you."

"I don't think it worked."

"Omar likes you."

"Bahar doesn't."

"No." Adam sighs. "He says he expects this from Magdi but not from me."

"Does this change anything? Between us, I mean."

"I don't know."

His answer takes me by surprise, not at all what I was expecting. I pull away and sit up. Adam shifts beside me, threading his fingers through mine. "You must understand," he says. "Bahar has been my friend for a very long time and his opinion is important to me."

If Hannah didn't approve of my boyfriend, I would seriously reconsider my life choices. So I can't fault Adam for wanting his friend's blessing. Still, it hurts—both that Bahar doesn't like me and that his opinion gives Adam room for doubt.

"So what do we do?"

The captain produces a cold meze plate with various dips, cheeses, olives, and bread, and I can't help but think his timing was intentional. Adam's reply is forgotten and I don't press because I don't think either of us has the answer. Instead we eat, watching Cairo drift past. On the water, the temperature feels almost cool and the city almost quiet. Soon our problems seem miles away.

"A felucca ride on the Nile is very romantic," I say. "Are you trying to woo me?"

"What is 'woo'?"

"Trying to make me like you."

His eyebrows hitch up and he gives me a little smirk. "Already you like me."

"Yes, I do." We look at each other for a long time and even though the temptation to kiss him hangs between us, I don't reach for it. There's something so satisfying about just taking in his soft, dark curls and the way his smirk has melted into a shy smile under the weight of my gaze. "I like you very much."

He tucks a strand of my hair behind my ear and a shiver follows his fingers, zipping down my spine like an electrical current. "I feel the same."

Despite being shielded from the eyes of the city, we don't kiss. We feed each other bites of hummus and baba ghanoush. We talk until we run out of words and voices to speak them, sharing the small details we don't know about each other—birthdays, broken bones, and best memories. We fall asleep in the shade, my head against his shoulder and my arm around his waist.

Adam is still sleeping when I wake and I try to commit his profile to memory because we are living on borrowed time. Soon his father will be fully recovered and Adam will go back to work. We've started something we won't be able to finish.

"You are thinking very hard." He taps his finger on the end of my nose, bringing me back.

"Trying to figure out what you've got planned next," I lie.

"You will never guess," he says. "But I am thinking twice about going back to land. I have never had such a relaxing day."

"Maybe we could just sail away."

He strokes my hair, his hand coming to rest against the side of my neck. "Such a good dream."

Stepping off the felucca feels like stepping back to reality and I don't much care for it. Except Adam bristles with excitement and I can't help but catch it. He tells me we're going to a place called Saqiat El Sawy. "In English it means El Sawy Culture Wheel; it is a place of music, art, and film. Every day they have events, and tonight we will hear my favorite band."

The entrance to the Culture Wheel is tucked beneath the 15th May Bridge in Zamalek, so I am expecting it to be a tightly packed little venue like some of the places we go to back home. But the complex stretches along the river, boasting several performance halls, open-air concert spaces, and a café-style seating area near the water. The whole place gives off an industrial vibe, but small trees and patches of grass here and there soften the effect, increase the charm. And the lights strung along the Nile cast a golden glow. It feels . . . magical.

There are several events happening at once—a puppet show, a calligraphy workshop, a poetry recitation, and a Japanese hula dance exhibition—but we are here to see an Egyptian reggae band. And when we enter the concert hall, Adam's friends are waiting for us. All except Bahar.

"I would *never* have guessed reggae," I say.

Adam grins. "Did I not say this?"

"You did, but I'm still surprised."

"A lot of us like reggae, rap, indie, and we even listen to American pop music," Hasnah says. "If anything, be surprised that heavy metal shows usually draw the biggest crowds at the Culture Wheel."

She isn't mean about it, but I still feel embarrassed that I bought into a musical stereotype just because Adam's dad listens to Arabic music in the car. Adam keeps the radio off when he drives (one less distraction), so I wouldn't have a clue about his tastes—or what kind of music people his age might like.

As the band takes the stage, I am deflated. Like I messed up with Adam's friends. Magdi grabs Hasnah by the hand and twirls her, making her giggle. Omar bobs his head to the rhythm and sings along. Reggae here is the same as reggae everywhere, but not knowing the words makes me feel even more outside. Adam and I together, alone, are perfect. We always have things to talk about, but around his friends I realize that I don't know very much at all. I can't stop myself from wondering if he'd feel the same way around my friends.

Adam leans into me, his mouth beside my ear. "This song is about a small house, a poor house where the mother all the time worries about her family and the father doesn't know how he will feed his children. But also how people may have wealth to build a thousand houses but are poor inside." He taps his chest. "Their hearts are small houses."

"I wish I understood." I'm not sure if I'm talking about the language or his friends. Probably both. I want to fit in.

"With time you will," he says, and I smile because he doesn't know that he read my mind—again.

From the other side of the floor, Hasnah beckons us to come dance. Everyone is moving and the day has been too good to waste what's left, so I take Adam's hand and lead him over. By the time the band has finished their set, my hair is damp, my shirt is sticking to my back, and I have at least one thing in common with Adam's friends.

We say good-bye to them with hugs and cheek kisses. Omar gives me a friendly wave. Hasnah takes my phone number and suggests we get together without Magdi and Adam. I tell her I like that idea.

"This day," I say as Adam and I walk through the Culture Wheel, bathed in the glow of the string lights. A breeze blows in off the river, cooling my skin. "I can't remember having a better day than this one."

After three years with Owen, I should have lots of memorable days—and I do—but this one is perfect. Until my phone rings and I hear a hint of panic in my mom's voice on the other end of the line. "Caroline, where are you?"

"Just leaving El Sawy Culture Wheel," I say.

"Oh, thank God."

"Mom, you're scaring me. What's wrong?"

"There was an attack on a clinic today in Libya. Not OneVision, but two doctors were killed and several people injured. I just—it's getting late and you aren't here, and I just wanted to hear your voice."

"I'm okay, Mom. I'll be home soon."

"I was going to ask if you wanted to have tea before we leave," Adam says. "But now we should go back."

I nod. "She sounds pretty shaken up, and with my dad not here . . ."

"I understand."

Even though we're in agreement that I need to get home, the drive goes too fast, and then we're outside my building too soon. Adam walks me into the vestibule and summons the elevator. When the doors are closed behind us, he pins me gently against the elevator wall, his fingers sliding into my hair as he kisses me. He runs his thumb across my lower lip, then follows with his mouth, a new move that makes me shiver. And when his tongue touches gently against mine, spontaneous combustion seems not only possible but imminent. We are both breathless when he pulls slowly away, releasing me just as the doors open.

In the hallway outside my apartment, I rest my forehead against his and keep my voice low so my mom and the neighbors won't hear. "Where did you learn to kiss like that?"

"From Nic—from American films."

"Wait. You were going to say Nicholas Sparks, weren't you?"

"Aya made me watch them," he protests, his cheeks coloring.

I laugh softly. "Them? Your sister forced you to watch multiple Nicholas Sparks movies?"

He silences me with another kiss, and how he learned doesn't matter anymore. The elevator grinds to a stop on my floor and we jump apart as the doors slide open. Masoud pokes his turbaned head out to survey the hallway. His eyes narrow when he sees us standing alone and he says something in Arabic.

Adam rolls his eyes. "He says it is time for me to go. So . . . good night."

He makes no move to leave, though, and I can't hold back a smile. "Night," I say. "Thanks again for today."

The way his cheek dimples when he smiles back is nearly as good as one last kiss. "If I could, I would give you every day like this one."

I slip quietly through the front door as Adam steps onto the elevator with the *bowab*, and I'm lucky I don't have to be part of *that* conversation. My mom leaps up from the couch as I enter the apartment and gathers me into a python squeeze hug. Her breath rushes past my ear, as if she's been holding it until I got home. She relaxes against me and I can almost feel her tension drain away.

"Are you okay?" I ask.

"Sometimes I think bringing you here was a mistake." She untangles from me and scrubs the heel of her hand against her eyes, wiping away tears. "Putting myself in danger is one thing, but—"

"Mom, everything's fine. I'm safe."

"Maybe you should go back to Ohio."

A small bubble of panic wells up inside me. My time in Cairo already has an expiration date that's too soon. I don't want to leave sooner. "You're overreacting."

"Maybe you're right." She strokes my hair back with her hand and kisses my forehead. "Let's get some sleep. We'll talk about this more when your dad gets home."

CHAPTER 21

Sleep? Ha! I'm still floating in a bubble of happiness as I log in to my video chat with Hannah. Except there's a guy sitting beside her, sporting a buzz cut and impressive biceps, both of which surprise me. Hannah is usually attracted to guys who are kind of scrawny, but Vlad is built like a wall. He's a great-looking wall, though.

"I hope you don't mind," she says. "I wanted you to meet each other."

The truth is, I wanted to talk to her about today and about Adam. But as Vlad waves and says hello to me through the computer screen, Hannah beams at his profile like he's the greatest thing since pizza. I know *exactly* how she feels right now, so I set aside what I want and wave back. "Hi there. I don't mind at all."

For the next ten minutes I play third wheel as they talk, mostly to each other. Hannah is gentle in the way she corrects Vlad's grammatical mistakes and it's clear by his effort to get everything right that he wants to impress her. Language is the only barrier between them and they're overcoming it. I envy that so much.

From the other room comes the jingle of keys and the click of the front door closing. Dad's here.

"Hey, Hann," I interrupt. "I'm so sorry to cut this short, but my dad just walked in the door. Since I haven't seen him in a while—"

"Go," she says. "Love you to the moon."

"And back."

Dad comes into my room as I close the laptop. He looks exhausted from traveling but envelops me in an extra-big hug. "You're up late."

"I was just talking to Hannah," I say. "I'm glad you're home."

"That makes two of us, kid." He ruffles my hair. "I've missed you. Maybe while I'm home you can show me around?"

"Definitely."

Sleep feels so far away as I fall into bed, and the day swims through my head like a dream I don't want to forget. I wonder if Adam sleeping or if he's thinking about me, too.

When I finally wake the next day, Mom has a plan in place. She's taken the day off from the clinic and called Adam to drive us to the Khan.

Aside from a quick hello, Adam and I can't really talk to each other in the car—at least not the things we want to say. I sit with my mom in the back, try not to stare at him in the rearview mirror, and hope my heart isn't glowing like neon on my sleeve. When we reach the bazaar, I'm disappointed when Mom arranges a time for him to pick us up and sends him on his way.

As we walk through the Khan, my mom tells Dad and me about some of her more problematic patients—people who come with broken bones and open sores, rather than eye problems—but playing on repeat in my head is the image of Adam kissing me in the elevator. It isn't until my parents go silent that I know I've missed something.

"What?"

"Are you even listening?" Mom asks.

"Sorry," I say. "I'm kind of hungry."

"Caroline, you ate breakfast."

"I know."

Although I'm not actually hungry, we stop at a street vendor for a plate of *fūl*. I show Dad how to pinch the bean mixture between pieces of bread, and he likes the dish so much that (fortunately for me) he eats almost the entire order.

"So I asked if you had any ideas about what we might bring Manar tonight as a hostess gift," Mom says as we resume our walk through the alleys and archways. "If we were in Ohio, I would take a bottle of good wine, but that won't work here. And the guidebooks all suggest chocolates, but we did that for Ahmed when he was in the hospital."

"Mrs. Elhadad was wearing a really pretty hijab when we met her," I say. "Maybe we could buy her a scarf. Or . . . everybody likes dessert. Maybe a cake?"

"Both," Dad says. "Get both."

We spend a couple of hours exploring the Khan and buying more decorations for the apartment, as well as some gifts for people back home, and I haggle successfully for a coral-colored scarf with metallic gold flowers embroidered along the edge. Perfect for Adam's mom. I pay attention as my mother talks about how her assistant has increased the number of male patients at the clinic and as Dad talks about how his boat spent a week of their hitch at the dock, waiting out a hurricane. I tell them both what I learned about the City of the Dead.

"I'd like to see that," Dad says.

"Some of my patients live there," Mom says. "Many of them need so much more than I can provide. I've been treating bug bites, respiratory infections, and minor illnesses. None of them seem to care that my specialty is ophthalmology."

Adam meets us at the Khan at the appointed time and

helps carry rugs, tapestries, and trinkets to the car. He stops at a bakery so Mom can buy a chocolate layer cake for Manar and, as he pulls up in front of our building, reminds us that he'll return at 8 p.m. to pick us up for dinner. Even though I know it's his job to drive us around, Adam is my friend now—more than a friend—and it's uncomfortable treating him like an employee. As I slide across the backseat toward the door, our eyes meet in the rearview mirror and he scrunches up his nose, making me laugh.

My parents are still in the bathroom—Dad finishing his shower, Mom blow-drying her hair—when the doorbell rings. I close my bedroom door so they won't be able to see the mountain of clothes I built while trying to find the perfect outfit for dinner with Adam's family. Even though I've already met them, I still want to make a good impression.

"I've got it," I call out as I open the front door.

Adam is dressed in a pair of navy chinos and a white button-up shirt with the cuffs rolled. Freshly shaved, curls damp, and smelling like soap. The sight of him stops me in my tracks. His gaze slides from my bun to my sandals—in exactly the same way as some of the other Egyptian guys I've encountered—but there's nothing annoying about Adam's attention. It makes me glad I went with my favorite white maxi dress with light-and-dark-blue-watercolor stripes and a navy cardigan. We kind of match, which sends a little thrill through me.

"Wow. Hi." I glance toward the bathroom, where Mom's blow-dryer is roaring, then tilt my face up to steal a kiss. Risky but *so* worth it. "You look exceptionally handsome right now."

He touches my chin, kisses my forehead, and says, "You look exceptional always."

The blow-dryer switches off and I step back, inviting him all the way into the apartment. Adam sits on the couch while I choose the chair, so when Mom emerges from the bathroom a moment later, heels clicking on the hardwood, we're the picture of propriety.

"Casey's just about ready," she says as she goes into the kitchen for the cake.

Since bright colors, dress clothes, and my dad don't really mix, he comes into the living room wearing a dark gray button-up shirt and black jeans. His Doc Marten shoes are buffed to a shine. With his sleeves rolled down and buttoned at the wrist, the only tattoo that really shows is the one around his ring finger. As a newly married deckhand, he nearly lost that finger when his wedding band got caught on the boat engine, so he traded it for permanent ink.

"You clean up pretty nice," I say.

Mom hands him the cake and gives him a lingering kiss. "Very sexy."

I grimace at the parental PDA, making Adam laugh.

"How terrible it must be to have parents who love each other." Dad ushers us out the front door.

I grin at him. "It's the worst."

"Listen, kid, if you find someone you love half as much as I love your mom, you should consider yourself lucky."

What I feel for Adam Elhadad can't be love—that would be crazy—but when I glance at him from the corner of my eye and he smiles at me, the butterflies in my stomach go wild. And I consider myself pretty lucky.

CHAPTER 22

The Elhadads' apartment is on a residential street lined with apartment towers. The streets are narrow with no houses or trees. And while the buildings aren't crumbling like the apartments in Manshiyat Nasr, they're also not upscale like our place in Manial. Adam leads us to a brick building where the *bowab* is a skinny, bearded man who sits on a kitchen chair beside the door. At his elbow is a tiny table with a glass of tea and a cigarette burning in an ashtray. When he speaks to Adam, there are holes in his mouth where some of his teeth should be. Adam gestures toward us as he replies. The man says something else as he opens the door for us, but Adam shakes his head in refusal.

"In most things, Gaber is a help," Adam says as we climb the first flight of steps. "But he demands fifty piastres from each person to operate the lift. Since my family lives on the second floor, we take the stairs. *Alhamdulillah* we don't live on the eighth floor."

At the top of the second flight we enter the hall and follow Adam to the first door on the left. He knocks, identifies himself, and—after waiting a beat or two—enters. Mr. Elhadad is first to greet us, and he looks more robust than the last time we saw him. The color has returned to his face and his eyes are bright again.

He welcomes us to his home. Cheek kisses are exchanged. Gifts are offered and thanks given. Shoes are left at the door. Adam excuses himself back into the hall. And then we are swept into a small, formal living room packed with furniture. Old-fashioned gold-and-crystal chandeliers dangle from the ceilings, casting a warm glow over the room.

"Your home is lovely," Mom says as Mrs. Elhadad brings in a tray of tea for the adults. Aya follows behind with Pepsi for herself, Adam, and me. She greets everyone in the room, then sits beside me on the couch. She's wearing a pair of loose-fitting khakis with a wide brown belt, a long-sleeved green-and-white striped top, and a green hijab with tiny black polka dots. I touch her sleeve. "Is your wardrobe ever not on point?"

Our families make small talk over a plate of *feteer* filled with cheese and figs, and a feta cheese dip made with cucumbers and fava beans. Mr. Elhadad tells us he is ready to drive again and I wonder if Adam is as disappointed as I am. What will he do now?

He returns with an older lady dressed in an unadorned chestnut-brown dress. Instead of wearing a hijab, she has her gray hair pulled back in a low bun. The men stand to welcome her, and Mr. Elhadad introduces her as his mother, Nazeerah, and explains that her English is limited. As they fall back into conversation, Mr. Elhadad translates and Mom speaks as much Arabic as she can.

Adam takes a seat across from me and I want to ask if this is the grandmother who taught him how to cook, if he prepared any of the food for tonight's dinner, and if he's already looking for a new job. But asking him these questions in front of his family feels too intimate. Instead I scoop a bit of the cheese dip onto a cracker and give him a quick smile before looking away.

After a couple rounds of tea, Mr. Elhadad invites us to the dining room for a spread of roasted chicken with potatoes; a salad of marinated green beans, beets, and carrots; and dishes of pickled cucumbers. It's not fancy food, but it looks and smells delicious. It reminds me of Sunday dinner with Grandma Irene, who serves garlic mashed potatoes and homemade chunky applesauce with her roasted chicken.

"Now," Mr. Elhadad says to Dad when we're all settled

around the table. "I would like it if you would explain your job to my wife and my mother." Since my father has never walked away from an opportunity to talk, he speaks at great length about life aboard a tugboat, pausing only to let Mr. Elhadad's translation catch up. Mom asks Mrs. Elhadad about being a seamstress. Even Nazeerah contributes to the conversation, speaking in Arabic about how she used to work as a maid for a wealthy Cairene family.

"I bet you'll be glad to let your dad take over the driving again," Mom says to Adam. "Have you started looking for a new job?"

"I had an interview today at the Nile Ritz-Carlton," he says, and my heart lifts a little, thinking maybe losing the *koshary* shop wasn't too big a setback. Working in the kitchen at the Ritz-Carlton sounds like it might be an improvement. "I begin as a waiter on Saturday."

Mrs. Elhadad says something and her husband explains that they are proud of him, that a waiter can earn a good income.

"But that's not your dream." The words spill out, even though I'd meant for them to stay in. And when I look up from my plate of chicken, seven pairs of eyes—even those of the elder Mrs. Elhadad, who probably didn't understand what I said—are on me. "I just meant . . . you should be working in a kitchen. You should be cooking."

"It is a good job." Adam speaks to the whole table, but I know he's trying to reassure me. And convince himself. "I can take the metro almost to the front door."

Mr. Elhadad's gaze bounces from me to Adam to his wife, and I see the subtle downturn at the corners of her mouth. When she notices I'm watching her, Mrs. Elhadad gives me an awkward smile and offers me the bowl of salad for a second helping. My own parents glance at each other with concerned eyes, and my humiliation level redlines. I blink back tears as I dish a couple more carrots onto my plate, and Dad launches into a story about how, at eighteen, he was fired from waiting tables because he broke too many dishes. I'm pretty sure he made up the story just now to help Adam feel better and that makes it even harder not to cry.

The conversation moves on and I spend the rest of the dinner focused on my food. Taking more when it's offered, even when I'm full. When Mrs. Elhadad brings out after-dinner coffee, Aya says she has something she wants to show me and I follow her gratefully away from the dining room.

"How embarrassed should I be right now?" I say as she closes her bedroom door. The pale purple walls are covered with pencil sketches and finished colored drawings of hijabi fashion. An ancient-looking sewing machine stands in one corner of the room, while in the other corner is a tall, narrow shelving unit in the corner that is almost completely filled with rolled scarves in every color.

"My family will wonder how you know about my brother's dreams and perhaps they have guessed he has shared them with you, but on Saturday everything returns to normal," she says, flopping onto her bed. "Everything will be forgotten."

Including me?

Her room goes blurry with fresh tears.

"It's not so bad." Aya hands me a tissue. "My parents cannot say that Adam must work as your driver, then be angry when he speaks to you."

"He kissed me."

"Oh." She covers her mouth with her hand for a moment, then says, "Was it like a movie?"

I laugh as I wipe my eyes. "Actually, it was."

Aya is silent for a while, considering. "Maybe that can be enough?"

"Maybe." I touch one of the drawings on her wall. It's a picture of the outfit she was wearing at the hospital when I met her. "Adam told me about this. You have so much talent. Why do you want to study engineering when you could be doing this?"

"My family is happy, but there is never a time when we do not struggle," she says. "I am not like my brother. My dream can wait until I am no longer poor."

"That's very practical," I say, feeling fortunate—yet again—that I don't have to be practical with my future. Even if I risk it on an anthropology or history degree, I still have a better chance of earning more money in the United States than Aya will in Egypt.

"It's good to dream," she says. "But better to have a plan."

I walk over to her hijab collection and choose one that is the rich, dark blue of Lake Erie in November. My favorite color. Aya takes the fabric from me. "I will show you how to wrap a hijab . . . well, there are many ways to do it, but I will show you one."

She repositions my bun so it sits at the back, rather than on top, then places the scarf over my head. Aya pins the tails beneath my chin, then drapes one of the tails around my neck, arranging the fabric into neat folds. She brings the other tail over my head, letting it hang down beside my face and pinning it into place so it won't slip.

Without my hair showing, my identity feels lost and the dark blue fabric makes my face look washed-out. Not like Aya, who looks so beautiful wearing a hijab. I crinkle my nose at the reflection in the mirror. "It's not me."

"It takes time to get used to it, and I think such a dark blue is not your color," Aya says. "I chose to wear the hijab when I was twelve, so I have learned how to wrap it in ways that are good for my face, and darker colors need bolder makeup. We all have bad hijab days sometimes."

"Is that why not every woman in Egypt wears one?" I ask.

"The choice is personal," Aya says. "Of course, there are people who believe every woman should cover, but if I decide not to wear my hijab, no one can force me."

My mind goes back to the women at the airport on my first day in Cairo and it makes more sense now. I still don't understand why anyone would choose to hide her face, but I guess another woman's choice is not really my business.

Aya removes the scarf from my head and plaits a few tiny braids into my hair before she does it back up in the topknot.

"Adam told me how you used to braid his hair when you were kids," I say, rolling the hijab into a neat bundle before putting it back on the shelf.

She sighs. "I have always wished for hair like his. He washes it and it dries into perfect curls, while I must use a curling wand to get the same results. It's unfair."

Not wanting to think about Adam's hair, I change the subject. "We haven't really had much chance to hang out. I was thinking . . . would you be interested in joining a club with me?"

"What sort of club?"

"I'm not sure," I say. "Maybe a sport?"

The Elhadads' computer is in the main living area, so we use our phones to look up women's sports teams in Cairo.

"There's a roller derby league," I say, and I can picture myself on a flat track, knocking skaters out of my way and having a really awesome derby name like Vivi Section or Abbey Roadkill. The reality, though, is that my strongest roller skating skill is falling down.

Aya shakes her head. "I am not cool enough for roller derby and I don't think my parents wish for me to die."

I laugh. "Fair enough. What about rugby?"

"What is that?"

"Okay, no rugby."

Finally we discover a recreational women's soccer team called the Garden City Daffodils, founded by a couple of expatriates— one American, one Australian. According to their website, they compete against teams from the area sporting clubs. Joining this team would be good conditioning for my high school team tryouts in September. And maybe help keep my mind off Adam.

"I can do this," Aya says. "I would like to do this."

We fill out the contact form on the team's website, then hang out in her room until Adam's fingers drum softly on the door and he tells us to come out for dessert.

CHAPTER 23

Midnight closes in as Adam drives us across the bridge to Manial after an uneventful serving of chocolate layer cake and a heaping of thanks on my mother for her part in saving Mr. Elhadad's life. Adam stops at our building and it feels final somehow. Especially when Dad hands him a big tip and wishes him good luck with the new job.

"*Shokran,*" Adam says quietly.

Mom thanks him for keeping me company.

"*Afwan,*" he says.

There is so much I want to say, but not now, not in front of my parents. I follow them toward the building, but after taking a few steps, I pause and look back. Adam is still there. He smiles and touches his hand to his heart.

Upstairs, standing on the balcony, I send him a text. **Are we finished?**

I don't want to be.

Will I see you tomorrow?

Adam doesn't respond right away, but when I look over the railing, his father's car is still down there on the street. Finally my phone chimes.

Yes.

"I'm a little concerned about Caroline." Mom's voice drifts out onto the balcony from my parents' bedroom. I step back as she closes the doors for privacy, then creep into the shadow between their room and mine. Her voice is more muffled now, but I can still hear it when she says, "She and Adam . . . well, they seem . . . attracted to each other."

"That was pretty evident from day one."

"They've been spending a lot of time together," Mom says. "And when I spoke to Manar about it, she said he has been miserable."

"Of course he is, Beck," Dad says. "He's head over heels for a girl—probably for the first time in his life—and has no idea how to deal. His culture says one thing, but his hormones are singing a completely different, much louder song. And now his access to her is about to get cut off. They're probably both pretty miserable right now."

"Doesn't that bother you?"

"Why should it?"

"Because the boy isn't supposed to be spending time with Caroline, let alone developing feelings for her."

"That's between Adam and his faith," my dad says. "Not my business. But what I do know is that he's a good kid and so is our daughter. She dated Owen for three years, so what's different now?"

"I don't want her to lead him astray."

Dad laughs a little. "He may be Muslim, but he's still a guy. She isn't leading him anywhere he isn't willing to go. But look, Ahmed is back on his feet, I'm here now, and we've got that school orientation thing coming up, right? She'll meet some of her new classmates, and Adam will get her out of his system. Problem solved."

I slip out of the shadows and into my room, where I lie in the dark for a long time wondering if Dad is right.

The early morning light is seeping into my room when I receive a text from Adam telling me he's on his way. I shower and dress in record time, pulling my damp hair into a bun. Mom comes out of her bedroom wearing her pajamas as I'm headed for the front door.

"Where are you going?"

"My driver is coming to pick me up," I say. "Not sure where we're going or when we'll be back, though. Leading Muslim boys astray takes time."

Her eyebrows arch up. "Were you eavesdropping?"

"When you can overhear it . . . it's called overhearing."

"Then you know the context," she says. "I don't want to see either of you get hurt, but there is a lot more at stake here for Adam than there is for you. The kind thing to do would be to leave him alone."

Dad shuffles out of the bedroom, scratching the back of his head. "Why are we all awake right now?"

"Tomorrow Adam starts his new job," I say to Mom. "And then he'll have all the time in the world to *get me out of his system*. Problem solved, right?"

My dad winces as I throw his words back at him. "Listen, Caroline—"

"No." I hold up a hand to stop him. "You brought me here. You expected me to make the best of it in a strange country. Adam *is* the best of it and I am one hundred percent done with this conversation."

I yank open the front door.

"Caroline Elizabeth Kelly, stop right now," Mom demands, but I walk out, slamming the door behind me.

I hate that my parents and Bahar are on the same team. I

hate that being with Adam feels right and wrong at the same time. It can't be both. Rebellion has never suited me, but my heart and mind are a tangled mess. Still, the elevator is barely past the second floor when I send my parents an apology text. **Sorry for being a jerk. Adam and I just need time to talk.**

Adam is waiting at the curb. "How are you?"

"I don't know."

We don't talk as the car winds through the streets of the city. I want to ask him what he is thinking, but I'm scared of the answer. There are dark circles under his eyes, as if he didn't get much sleep, and I wonder what happened at his apartment last night after we left. Adam takes me to our first *ahwa*, the one in Coptic Cairo, where it is quiet and private.

"I am Muslim." Adam looks over my shoulder instead of looking me in the eye. "And you are not. You are leaving Cairo in a year and this is my home."

"That sounds like someone else talking."

"While I was driving you and your parents home, my whole family came together—aunties, uncles, cousins—and when I returned, they all had opinions to share, very loudly and very late into the night," he says as the waiter brings tea and *karkadeh*. "They believe that if I am old enough to be thinking of you in a romantic way, then perhaps it is time for me to be married."

"What do *you* believe?"

"I am Muslim." He rotates his coffee glass one way, then the other. Stalling. He clears his throat. "This is what I meant that first day in the park. I thought—well, I closed my eyes and pretended it would be different for us. There is no future in which we live happily ever after."

My heart burns and I want him to hurt as badly as I do. "Maybe you *should* get married. Have a bunch of kids and spend the rest of your life living in the same apartment building as your mother, dreaming about how you might have been a chef."

My poisoned words hit their mark and pain registers across Adam's face, except hurting him makes me feel even worse. Especially since I used his culture and hardship against him. Getting married, having kids, and living near his mother isn't a bad alternative fate at all. It's a normal Egyptian fate.

Before I can take back the insult, the warmth drains from his eyes and he lifts his shoulders in a careless shrug. "Perhaps instead I should turn my back on my family and faith for a girl who can never be anything but temporary."

My chest feels torn open and hollowed out as I scoot back my chair. The table wobbles, spilling my drink, and the red liquid cascades over the edge onto the cobblestones. "I'm going home."

"Caroline, wait."

Tears burn in my eyes because I still love the way he says my name, but the pain pushes my feet forward. "Go away, Adam."

"It is a long walk and a hot day. Let me drive you."

I don't want to be in the same city with him, let alone the same car. "No."

"Please." The crack in his voice is all it takes to make me get in the car, but the air is heavy between us. I want to apologize, but all I can think about is how I am a temporary girl. By the time we reach my building, the opportunity feels lost.

As I reach for the door handle, Adam leans across the console and cradles my face with both hands. His kiss is a desperate plea and I let him make it. The second time, I kiss him back, tasting the good-bye on his lips the same way I taste the salt of my tears. But the thought of not having a tomorrow with Adam hurts more than the terrible things we said to each other.

"If I could be more like Magdi . . . ," he says.

I sniffle and laugh at the same time. "I'm so glad you're not."

"*Bahebik.*"

I open the door. "What does that mean?"

Adam's smile is sad. "Already you know."

I pass Masoud for the second time this morning and he holds up his Quran, silently scolding me. My middle finger itches to aim itself in his direction but instead—even though he doesn't understand a single word—I say, "Save it for someone who cares."

CHAPTER 24

Mom is dressed for work as I come into the apartment, and when she sees the tears staining my cheeks, she wraps me up tightly in her arms. "Are you okay?"

"No," I say to her shoulder.

"You did the right thing."

"Please don't. Not now."

She kisses my forehead. "I'm so sorry."

I untangle from her embrace and hide out in my room, crawling beneath the covers, where I cry myself to sleep. Mom is long gone when I wake, and Dad's sitting on the balcony with his laptop and his Deadpool mug filled with coffee.

"Hey there, Bug," he says.

When I was about three or four, I invented a game I called

Lightning Bug where I'd dance around the room and pretend to flash. Dad would "catch" me in an imaginary jar and after I made a sufficiently sad face, he'd set me free and the game would start over. He took to calling me Lightning Bug and over the years the nickname became abbreviated to Bug.

Below us the city keeps moving noisily forward. "Hey."

"Thinking about going for a walk," he says. "Wanna come?"

I'd really rather not do anything at all, but my dad's time in Cairo is not unlimited. "Yeah, okay."

Mom believes that talking about your feelings is healthy, which is probably true, but one of the things I love best about Dad is that he knows when *not* to talk. His philosophy is that sometimes the only way to get over feeling like shit is to feel like shit.

We cross the road and walk south along the river. No one hassles me when I'm with Dad. A couple of guys stare too long and he growls at them like a dog, making me laugh. By the time we reach the southern tip of the island about twenty minutes later, I'm feeling . . . not exactly good, but not quite so bad.

"I was doing some reading up on our island," Dad says. "And down here at this end is one of the last remaining nilometers, used in ancient times to measure the yearly flood levels. Let's check it out."

The nilometer looks kind of like a church steeple without a

church, sitting on top of a low stone building in the middle of a landscaped, green park at the very tip of the island. There are no tourists around and Dad offers the caretaker a small baksheesh to let us go inside, where a series of stone steps lead down into an empty well. Running up the middle of the structure is a stone pillar with markings carved at intervals. The whole thing reminds me of one of those M.C. Escher optical illusion drawings where the stairs seem to go two directions at once.

"The water levels were measured in cubits," Dad says. "Twelve or thirteen cubits meant hunger and suffering. Basically, drought conditions. Fourteen to sixteen was an indication that it would be a happy, abundant year. Eighteen or more was a flood disaster."

The caretaker takes us down the stairs to the bottom of the empty well. Above us, the steeple-like top lets in the light. The man holds up three fingers. "Three tunnels bring water into the nilometer," he says. "Now closed up. No more."

Dad explains that dams and reservoirs control the flooding now, minimizing the risk of disaster. The nilometer is pretty impressive in terms of ancient technology and architecture. It's beautiful and has lasted for more than a thousand years, but watching my dad geek out over this stuff is more entertaining than the actual building.

Afterward we stand on the terrace, looking down the Nile as cruise boats, fishing skiffs, and feluccas drift past.

"So did you bring me here as some sort of metaphorical life lesson?" I ask.

He laughs. "Nope. I just wanted to spend some time with my girl. But if you're desperate, how about this: Sometimes life gives you an eighteen-cubit flood of unfairness and there's not a *damn* thing you can do about it."

"Did you just dad-pun me?"

"Hey, I thought that was a pretty good one."

I shoulder bump him, smiling in spite of myself. "Keep telling yourself that, Kelly."

On our way home, we pass a footbridge that crosses the narrow canal between the island and the rest of the city. We cross, and when we reach the other side, I discover we're only a few blocks from Coptic Cairo. I tell him about how Adam took me to the Hanging Church. "Do you want to go?"

"Let's save that for our next wander," Dad says. "I need to buy some flowers before your mom gets home from work. We're having a date night. Without you."

"'Date night' kind of implies that."

"You gonna be okay?"

"Maybe you could have Masoud babysit," I say, which makes him crack up laughing.

The *bowab* is waiting for us when we get home. He gets up from his little stool when he sees us coming and presents me with a birdcage. Inside is a green bird with a rosy-colored face and bright, lively eyes. *"Min alshshab,"* the *bowab* says, pushing both his disapproval and the cage at me. *"Min alshshab."*

"Do you have any idea what he's saying?" I ask Dad. "Or why I am now in possession of a bird?"

"Maybe *shab* means bird."

Masoud shoves a crumpled paper bag at me, then presses the button to bring down the elevator. As the three of us stand in awkward silence, waiting for it to come, the *bowab* eyes me with disdain. I think if he had his Quran, he'd shake it at me again.

"Shokran," I say when the elevator doors open, but not even politeness and a smile can crack the old nut.

Once the doors are closed, I open the paper bag to find bird pellets, food and water dishes, a couple of wooden toys, and a note: "No goats at al-Gomaa today."

I touch the paper to my lips, trying to keep from smiling. Failing to keep from smiling.

"It's from Elhadad, isn't it?"

"It is."

"A lovebird."

"Yep."

"You know"—Dad rubs the back of his head—"your mom and I . . . well, it's our job to protect you from the hard knocks this world can dish out. But maybe this isn't something we can protect you from. Maybe we need to let you and Adam figure things out for yourselves."

"It's too late for that," I say. "But thanks."

The lovebird's new home is on top of my dresser, where she (he?) has an elevated view of the room. After I hang the toys and fill the dishes with food and water, I look up *shab* on the Internet. It means "young man." *Min alshshab*. From the young man. Masoud's disapproval makes sense. A gift from the young man who should not be buying me gifts.

I send the young man a text. **I like birds better than goats.**

CHAPTER 25

Mr. Elhadad is back in action the next day, driving my family to a summer open house at my new school. It's located in a suburb of Cairo that looks relatively young. Out here, beyond Mokattam, there are villas with their own yards and new apartment buildings in various states of incompleteness. The school campus is modern and professionally landscaped with palms and immature shade trees, and we are greeted by the administrative team at the front door before being ushered into the auditorium.

"Pretty swanky place." Dad fiddles with the shirt button at his wrist. Salty language and tattoos are standard issue among the guys on his boat, and my dad doesn't care what conclusions people draw about him based on his ink. But he says he never wants Mom and me to be judged by his life choices. "I feel like we might be dragging down the property value."

According to the school's website, most of the students are Egyptian and the rest of us are the children of ambassadors, corporate CEOs, and expatriates from around the world. Even though my parents can afford the tuition, we're definitely not on the upper end of the socioeconomic scale.

There are about a hundred students in the senior class—a little more than at my small school in Ohio—and a few turn to look in our direction. I wonder if they've all known each other for years or if some of them are new like me.

The director gives a standard-issue welcome speech before sending us off to tour the campus. The classrooms are pretty much the same as any other classroom, but the teachers are as multicultural as the student body, which is different for me. My old school was predominantly white, predominantly Catholic.

Mom introduces herself to each of my teachers and proudly tells the soccer coach that I started on varsity as a freshman. She knows I have to try out for this team, but that doesn't stop her from giving him the full rundown on my high school career. I kick a ball to my dad. He traps it with his knee and sends it back, giving it enough lift for me to head it. We mess around like this until Mom is done bragging.

"I'm surprised you don't keep my soccer résumé in your purse," I tease as we cross the field back to the main building.

"He'll remember who you are," Mom says.

"Yeah, the American girl with the pushy mother."

Dad snickers, making her laugh. "Maybe I got a little carried away," she admits. "I'm allowed to be proud of you."

"And your mom's memorized those stats for just such an occasion," he points out to me with a wink. "Don't pee in her Wheaties."

The whole student body regroups in the canteen for a buffet luncheon, a spread that's a mix of traditional Egyptian foods and "American" standards like fried chicken, sausage rigatoni, and french fries. As I dish a little *koshary* onto my plate, my thoughts drift to Adam. I wonder if he likes his new job. I wonder if he knows he'll make bank on tips, especially if he remembers to smile. I hope he's happy.

We share a table with a United States ambassador and his family, including a daughter in third grade and his son, Ethan, who will be a senior like me. Ethan's light brown hair is tall and swoopy on top, and his khakis are rolled at the ankles in a deliberately messy way. He looks like he's come from a photo shoot and his smile says he knows he's good-looking.

"How long have you been in Cairo?" Ethan asks as our parents exchange greetings and launch into small talk.

"About six weeks."

"Where do you live?"

"We're in Manial."

His eyebrows pull together as if I'd just told him we live on the moon. "Huh. That's different."

When we were scouting places to live in Cairo, we checked out villas and apartments in Maadi and Zamalek, where many expatriates live, and Garden City, where the embassies are located. All of them boasted quiet, leafy streets and lots of things to do, as well as proximity to other expatriates. But the rents were out of our reach, and Dad didn't really want to live anywhere that was heavily populated with Americans. I don't tell Ethan this, though.

"Our apartment is right across the street from the Nile," I explain. "My mom fell in love with the view."

"This is our last year," he says. "My dad's appointment ends right around the time I graduate and I can't wait to get out of here."

"Really? Why?"

"It's hot as balls—"

"Ethan, language," his mother says, her voice low and soft. He rolls his eyes and forges on. "There's nothing to do and everyone hates us because we're American."

"I don't think I've met anyone who hates me." I play innocent, even though I'm pretty sure Adam's mother is not my biggest fan. Or the tongue-clicking woman on the metro. Or Bahar. Or Masoud. (Okay, maybe I have met several people who hate me.) Except after the words leave my mouth, I realize it sounds like I'm flirting with Ethan.

He cocks his head and aims a sly grin at me. "I can see why."

His smoothness seems practiced, as if he tries on smiles every morning until he finds the one he thinks will be most devastating. Even without Adam as a comparison, Ethan Caldwell is totally not my type.

"A bunch of us are going sandboarding at the dunes at Fayoum next weekend," he says. "Do you want to come?"

The point of Mom's elbow against my arm encourages me to say yes. Last winter I went snowboarding with my friends. None of us had ever tried it before, so we did a lot of crash-landing in the snow. If sandboarding is anything like snowboarding, I'm already really good at falling down. "That sounds like fun."

Ethan programs my number into his phone, then excuses himself to go talk to a table full of his friends. My phone beeps with an inbound text. **Now you have my number. Use it any time.**

I head to the dessert table, stepping up beside a tall girl

about my age with dark skin and natural black curls spiraling down her back. "Any idea what's good?"

"Dude." She smiles. "Dessert. It's all good."

"True." I laugh, choosing a bowl of *om ali*—the Egyptian equivalent of bread pudding. Grandma Rose is the wizard of bread pudding, so I might be setting myself up for disappointment, but it's one of my all-time favorite foods.

"I'm Vivian. Senior. Originally from upstate New York." She gestures toward a table where her parents are talking with another family. "My dad works for a global management consulting firm, which is basically biz babble for helping companies make more money."

"I'm Caroline," I tell her as Vivian selects an Egyptian dessert that looks like pudding sprinkled with pistachios. "A new senior from Ohio. My mom runs a OneVision clinic in Manshiyat Nasr."

"So what's your thing?" she asks as I follow her outside. Some of the little kids have migrated to the playground, while the older ones sit at outdoor tables. We find an empty table. "Mine's volleyball."

"Soccer."

"Competition for positions on that team is tough," she says, and a new worry opens up in my head. I hope Aya and I will hear back from the Daffodils soon.

Vivian and I compare class schedules for the fall—we have only English in common—and talk about the colleges we're considering. "My dream school is NYU," she says. "I'm looking at Cornell and Skidmore, too."

"I like Kenyon, Denison, and Case Western in Ohio," I say. "But my mom went to medical school at Fordham. My dad was living in the Bronx at the time and she met him while she was there, so I think they can both see me going to Fordham."

"Can *you* see yourself going to Fordham?"

"After a year in Cairo, I feel like New York City will probably be a piece of cake."

"True," Vivian says. "Can't hurt to apply."

"Are you going sandboarding next weekend?"

"I wasn't invited." She hesitates a moment, then lowers her voice. "I'm not saying the kids here are racist, but it can be kind of cliquish along ethnic lines, and Ethan Caldwell tends to hang with his own, you know?"

"Really? I thought because the school is so diverse—I guess that's kind of naive, huh?"

Vivian nods. "Seems like the more money a person's family has, the less tolerant they are. And that applies all across the board."

"That sucks."

"Yep."

"What if I invited you?" I ask.

"If you ditch me when we get there, you don't get a second chance."

"Based solely on first impressions, I'm about a hundred percent certain I'd rather hang out with you than Ethan."

"Of course you would." Vivian cocks her head and flashes a very Ethan-like grin as she aims finger guns at me, cracking me up. Then, in her normal voice, she says, "So I guess I'm going sandboarding."

We swap phone numbers before going back inside to track down our parents. My mom is with Ambassador Caldwell, and both of them have their cell phones pressed to their ears. Mom is worrying her lower lip between her teeth.

"What's going on?" I whisper to Dad, who's standing beside Mr. Elhadad.

The room has gone unnaturally quiet.

"A couple of humanitarian aid outposts in the Sinai, including a OneVision clinic, were attacked by a group claiming allegiance to the Islamic State," my dad says. "The ambassador doesn't think we have cause to worry here in Cairo—his own kids are staying put for now—but your mom is on the phone with OneVision."

"Oh my God. Was anyone hurt?"

"That's what we're waiting to find out."

My eyes travel around the room. Some of the people look worried, others angry. Someone's father—a white man— wonders aloud why Muslims don't police themselves. Accusing eyes turn toward the Muslims in the room and the air feels combustible.

"Thank you," Mom says into her phone, drawing my attention back to her. "No one from OneVision was killed," she tells us. "But the other organizations lost several staff members and patients."

Ethan shakes his head. "This place sucks."

"I don't understand," I say. "Why kill people who are trying to help?"

"ISIS wants foreigners and all their influence out," Dad says.

"They oppose anyone who does not follow the law as they see it," Mr. Elhadad says. "Even Muslims. Terrorists make no exceptions for anyone who does not believe exactly as they do."

I think about asking him why Muslims don't come together to stop this from happening, but I think I already know what he would say. Too many people here in Cairo—and probably in all of Egypt and the other predominantly Muslim countries— are just trying to make ends meet. Their days are full and their wallets are not. And if the Egyptian government can't bring running water to every tap and electricity to every building, can they finance a war? Or maybe I'm wrong and these governments can afford war. Maybe not all Muslim governments see the Islamic State as a threat. Maybe some even sympathize with their aims. It's complicated, and I feel sad, fortunate, and a little bit ashamed that if things go wrong, my family has the option to just walk away.

CHAPTER 26

Dad and I spend nearly every day of the following week exploring Cairo. Monday, we cross the footbridge into Coptic Cairo, where I show him the Hanging Church and introduce him to *karkadeh*. We visit Tahrir Square on Tuesday to see the graffiti and I start to feel a little more seasoned. People stare at us, but no one dares say a word. My dad might have a lion heart, but he also has tiger fists. His father taught him and Uncle Mike that they should never start a fight but also never be afraid to finish one. According to the stories they tell when they're together, Dad and Uncle Mike finished their fair share of fights when they were young but now, not so much. It's comforting to know there isn't much that scares my dad.

Midweek we ride Line 1 of the metro to its southern terminus in Helwan and get off the train. It is just as noisy and dirty as the rest of Cairo, but as we look for a place to stop for a cold drink, we come to the entrance of a large Japanese garden.

"Didn't expect this," Dad says. "Should we check it out?"

Admission is two Egyptian pounds—the equivalent of about a quarter—so we go inside. The park is filled with bamboo trees, pagoda-style huts, meandering stone canals crisscrossed by Japanese bridges, and a pond surrounded by dozens of sitting Buddhas. Like a lot of things in Egypt, neglect has tarnished the park's shine, but it's still peaceful and beautiful. We stay for a couple of hours, taking pictures of some kids climbing all over a jolly-faced Buddha, watching Egyptian families pedal across a man-made lake in little foot-powered boats, and discovering a set of "hear no evil, speak no evil, see no evil" monkeys carved into the rock of the pond.

"What an oddball place," Dad says as we leave the park and head back toward the metro station. "I like it, though."

The *asr* prayer is being called, which means it's probably around three thirty. One of the things I've learned since we've been here is the names of the prayers and when they fall during the day. They've become kind of like the church bells back home. I know what time it is when I hear them. "That's kind of how I feel about Cairo. It gets under your skin. Kind of like . . . a tattoo."

Dad nods. "Some places have the ability to do that."

"You should bring Mom here on your next date night. I bet when the lanterns are lit, it's romantic."

The kind of relationship my parents have is the kind that people wish for, but it's weird for *me* to be jealous of them. I want to be here with Adam when the lanterns are lit. Sneak kisses under the bamboo. I need to quit thinking about him, but the memory of his mouth against mine is seared into my brain.

Just before the Helwan metro station, Dad stops at a street cart selling *coctel*, a parfait-like treat with strawberries, bananas, apples, mango, and yogurt. Supertasty. Except as we ride the subway home, the swaying of the car makes me queasy, a feeling that builds until my stomach gurgles and a sour taste rises into my mouth. When the train stops at the next station—I have no idea which one it is—the doors open and I shove my way out onto the platform just as the *coctel* makes a messy, splashy return. More than one commuter looks at me in disgust as they sidestep my sick, and the subway guard rushes over to scold me in Arabic, as if I puked on purpose. Ignoring him, Dad leads me up the steps to street level and hails a cab to take us the rest of the way home.

For the first several months of my life—while my mom was finishing her residency—Dad was my primary parent. He was working as a mate on a liftboat in the Gulf of Mexico but quit his job to take care of me. From the stories they tell, he sang the lullabies (which is good because Mom can't carry a tune), walked the floors with me when I wasn't sleeping through the night, and even took me to a mommy-and-me group at the library. I love my mother, but Dad is the parent I want when I'm sick. Back at the apartment, he doses me with medicine to stabilize my insides and keeps the bottled water flowing until my stomach settles enough to sleep.

"It's all my fault," he confesses when Mom comes home to find I've burned through an entire roll of toilet paper. My body hurts from heaving, because I still keep throwing up, even though there's nothing left. "Street food."

"What did you eat?"

Dad tells her about the parfait and she just shakes her head at him. "Fresh fruit is always iffy. Even if it's been washed and peeled, you have no idea if the person preparing it has clean hands."

"Lesson learned."

That's easy for him to say. His stomach is lined with cast iron, while mine feels like it's been turned inside out.

I'm feeling less vomity when Jamie arrives for dinner the next evening. Mom's assistant looks fresh out of medical school, with a prematurely receding hairline, a toothy smile, and a brand-new wife, Sarah, who has never been outside Oklahoma.

Jamie is as thrilled to be in Cairo as my mom was when she was first offered the clinic, but Sarah confesses that she is terrified of basically everything. "It's so hot and dirty, and just thinking about going outside overwhelms me. Jamie does the shopping because I am afraid to go out there without him. And . . . I miss my mom."

Dad occupies Sarah with tugboat tales while Mom and Jamie spend the whole dinner talking about eyeballs. I'm still a little zoned out, so I go to bed right after dessert, leaving the adults to linger over coffee. In the morning I feel well enough to go sandboarding. I am dressing for the trip when I receive an e-mail from the Daffodils inviting Aya and me to come practice with the team.

Mr. Elhadad arrives while I'm filling a thermos of coffee, and as we drive to pick up Vivian, I ask him how his family is doing. Subtext: How is Adam?

"Aya told us she would like to join the Garden City Daffodils." He chuckles at the name. "I will take you both to the practices. And my son . . . well. Sometimes we have to do things we do not enjoy. Life is not always fair. With time I think he will understand this."

Is Mr. Elhadad talking about Adam's new job or about me? Both? Unsure of how to respond, I ask him to say hello to Adam and to tell Aya I can't wait to play soccer with her.

"She is very excited," Mr. Elhadad says.

We pick up Vivian in Zamalek, a neighborhood on another island in the Nile that is filled with trees and freestanding homes. It feels more like Ohio than any neighborhood I've seen so far. Vivian lives in an enormous stone villa with wrought-iron balconies and black-painted lions guarding the front steps. "Palatial" comes to mind, and once she's in the car, Vivian confirms that sometimes it feels like living in a castle.

"On the other hand," she says, "it's kind of ridiculous. My brother and sister are both gone away to college so we don't need five bedrooms or a basement filled with empty rooms."

"Our apartment is pretty huge, too," I say. "Only two bedrooms but we have space we'll never fill."

Saying these words in front of Mr. Elhadad makes me want to cringe, especially after having been to his apartment, where the small rooms were crowded with furniture. Aya's bedroom could have fit inside mine. Mr. Elhadad doesn't seem to be paying any attention to us, though. He hums along with the radio until we arrive at the meeting site—a café in Giza not far from the pyramids.

Ethan comes over as we get out of the car. If he's bothered that I invited Vivian, he has enough manners to greet both of us. "I'm glad you came."

Before I can answer, Mr. Elhadad reminds me to text him

when we're on our way back to Giza tonight. "I will be waiting for you when you arrive."

"I will. Thanks."

Ethan gestures toward a line of dusty white Land Cruisers to carry all the students out into the desert. The SUVs have basketlike luggage racks on the roof filled with sandboards and coolers. "I've already staked out—"

"Have you brought enough sunscreen and water?" Mr. Elhadad interrupts. It's a dad-like question that makes Ethan snicker, but I'm touched by the concern. I know exactly where Adam gets his thoughtfulness.

"Yes, I have both. Thank you for bringing us out here."

"You know, my dad could probably recommend a better driver than the one you're using," Ethan says as we walk toward the Land Cruisers.

Vivian rolls her eyes at him. "Not everyone needs an armored embassy car with tinted windows and a gun-wielding American security guard behind the wheel. Some expats actually live here."

All our homes are bigger than the average Cairo apartment. We have drivers who take us anywhere we want to go. We can afford to eat in five-star restaurants (well, maybe Vivian and Ethan can) and take sandboarding trips into the desert. We exist in a well-protected bubble inside the city limits, but none of us actually knows what it's like to *live* in Cairo.

"I'm just saying that most drivers are paid to stay in the background." Ethan rakes his hand through his hair. "And his car is kind of . . . old."

"Who cares about the age of his car as long as it runs?" I glance back to make sure Mr. Elhadad hasn't overheard any of this conversation, but he's long gone. "Besides, I like that he doesn't stay in the background. He's nice."

I end up sandwiched between Vivian and Ethan in the back of the first SUV, with Ethan's friend Will sharing the front seat with our guide, Zayed. Vivian brought along a set of Trivial Pursuit cards and the four of us spend most of the drive challenging each other with the questions.

Although American culture has managed to span the distance to Egypt—even Zayed gets some of the answers right—it's still easier to talk to other Americans. We get our jokes, we understand our idioms, and no one needs to translate. I loved the challenge that came with talking to Adam, but this is effortless.

CHAPTER 27

*P*avement gives way to bumpy sand tracks, and the desert stretches to the horizon in every direction. Heat shimmers in the distance, but we never catch up to it. Finally we reach the dunes. When Vivian opens the car door, a smothering heat barrels in and there is no way my sunscreen is going to stand up to the blistering rays. At my closet this morning, I waffled between short- and long-sleeved T-shirts, but now I'm glad I went with long.

There is a breeze, but the air is too hot for the breeze to be cooling, and with it comes grains of sand that catch on our eyelashes and stick to our lips. Sunglasses protect our eyes, but I can taste the salty grit as it crunches between my teeth. Zayed laughs when Vivian brings the neck of her T-shirt up over her nose.

"By the time you are done sandboarding," he says, unloading

four boards from the roof of the SUV, "there will be no part of your body that hasn't been touched by sand."

She groans. "Remind me why I said yes to this."

"It's going to be fun," I say, scooping up one of the boards.

The sand on our bare feet is like stepping onto the beach on the hottest day of summer. We run up the dune as fast as we can, but the sand has no purchase and we slide backward several times on the way. By the time we reach the top, my shirt is soaked through with sweat and I'm surprised I don't have first-degree burn blisters on the soles of my feet.

Zayed explains that we can go down the dunes standing up— like snowboarding—or sitting down on the board, toboggan-style.

"I'll demonstrate," he says, slipping his bare feet under the straps on the sandboard. "Then you follow."

He crouches down and tips himself forward. Zayed carves along the face of the dune on his way to the bottom, kicking up a wake of sand behind him. This is not a mountain, so the trip doesn't take long, and when he glides to a stop, he turns. "*Yalla!*" he shouts up to us, his hands cupped around his mouth.

Ethan—holding a GoPro on a stick—shoots forward first, mimicking Zayed as he zigzags his way down, trailing his fingertips in the sand like a surfer as he skims to the bottom of the dune. He throws up victory arms when he doesn't fall. Will, on the other hand, does a crash-and-burn about midway down and rolls the rest of the way, his board sliding behind him. Vivian and I take a selfie together at the top with my phone, then go down the dune at the same time.

I stretch out my arms, trying to maintain my balance, as wind rushes past my ears. Sand peppers my face. And I fall on my butt almost immediately. Vivian makes it a few more feet before she wipes out too.

"Almost everyone falls," Zayed assures us as we gather at the bottom, regrouping before we run back up. "Sand is less predictable than snow."

We stay on the dune for a couple of hours, sliding, climbing, falling, and doing a whole lot of laughing. On our last run, Vivian and I borrow Ethan's GoPro to make a video of ourselves as we toboggan down together on her sandboard.

As we pile back into the Land Cruiser, my legs are rubber, the tops of my knees are pink with an oncoming sunburn, and my face aches from smiling. Out here in the desert, where there is no haze of pollution, the sky is so clear and bright it almost hurts to look. The contrast of blue against gold, where the sky touches land, makes me feel as if I am looking at a painting. My breath catches in my chest and I wish . . . I wish I could stop wishing that Adam was here for this.

"Doing okay?" Ethan asks, dropping an arm around my shoulders.

"Oh, um—yeah. It's just really beautiful."

"I guess not *everything* about Egypt sucks." He smiles. It would be a lot easier on my heart if I could like someone like Ethan Caldwell—someone American—but there's not much point in that if your heart isn't making the rules.

"Where are we going next?" I ask Zayed as the SUV bumps its way through the desert.

"Wadi Al-Hitan is called the Valley of Whales," he says. "An ocean once existed here millions of years ago, and excavations have revealed thousands of prehistoric whales and sharks, as well as petrified coral and mangroves."

We can get only so close to the Valley of Whales before we have to get out of the SUVs and trek the rest of the way. It feels as if we are exploring a science fiction landscape—the surface of an alien planet—and Zayed explains that the rock formations jutting randomly from the ground have been scoured for millennia by the sand-laced winds, carving them into strange shapes.

"That one looks like my dick," Will whispers, making Ethan snicker.

The dig site is also home to an outdoor museum, where the exhibits are excavated skeletons of *Basilosaurus* and *Dorudon* whales, both prehistoric and both millions of years old.

Zayed says the *Basilosaurus* was equipped with small legs and feet that were not big enough to support the weight of a fifty-foot whale. "Scientists believe it is an ancestor to modern whales, that their legs evolved away as whales stopped coming out of the water."

Vivian links her arm through mine. "As a science nerd, I'm not even going to pretend I don't think this is completely cool."

"Right?" I say.

"I want to discover something like this."

"What? Whales?"

"No. I don't know. Maybe the cure for an incurable disease or a species of fish no one has been deep enough in the ocean to find yet." Just then Ethan and Will smash into each other—chest bumping chest—pretending to be prehistoric fighting whales. Vivian laughs. "Or I could pinpoint when exactly boys become such idiots."

"Pretty sure they're born like that."

From the Valley of Whales we travel to Wadi El Rayan, a protected sanctuary composed of a pair of lakes joined by a short natural spillway and a series of small waterfalls. There we are invited to a Bedouin camp for a lunch of pit-barbecued lamb, rice, and vegetables. We team up for volleyball and a pickup game of soccer. We leap from the top of a waterfall into the spillway below. And at sunset we roast marshmallows over the campfire as the sun sinks behind the dunes.

The ride back to Cairo is quiet. All of us are exhausted, dirty, and sunburned, and Vivian falls asleep with her sand-dusted hair on my shoulder. On the other side of me, Ethan plays a game on his phone.

"If you want," he says, not looking up, "my driver can take you home. Save your driver from having to come out so late. Vivian too."

Ethan's turned out to be nicer than I expected, so I take him up on his offer. I text Mr. Elhadad to let him know I won't be needing a ride. Then, because I can't help myself (and clearly have not learned my lesson about these things), I text Adam. **I miss you.** As the SUV returns to pavement, I watch the screen, hoping to see the little bubble that means Adam is responding, but it never comes.

It's past ten when we unload ourselves and our backpacks from the Land Cruiser. The embassy driver is waiting, standing beside a shiny black BMW. My smelly body is unworthy of this kind of luxury, but the air-conditioning is glacial and there are bottles of water in the backseat cup holders.

"That was a good time," Ethan says as we pull out of the parking lot. He turns to Vivian. "We should have invited you to hang with us sooner."

She fluffs her hair, raining sand all over the seat. "Probably."

He laughs. "Want to come to Hurghada with us next weekend?"

"Who's us?" Vivian asks.

"Basically me and Will. Maybe Mohammed Aal, if he can talk his parents into letting him go."

"So you need girls?"

Ethan nods. "We need girls."

Vivian explains that Hurghada is a beachfront city on the Red Sea. "It's basically like the Egyptian equivalent of Florida," she says. "Beaches. Bars. Snorkeling."

"The flight's only about a hundred bucks," Ethan adds.

"I'll ask," I tell them, but I'm skeptical my parents will give me permission to fly to another part of Egypt with a bunch of teenagers. Even if I leave out the part about the bars, my dad is not that gullible.

Dad is watching a movie on his laptop when I get home. We haven't bought a television because the local programming is in Arabic, so everything we watch is online. Mom's asleep with her head on his thigh, and Dad hits pause as I come into the living room.

"Leave any sand in the desert?" he asks, eyeing my dirt-streaked clothes.

235

Just scratching my scalp sends a tiny avalanche of grit down the back of my neck. "Only what I couldn't carry home in my underwear."

Dad laughs through his nose. "Good time?"

"Yeah. It was," I say. "Got a ride home in an embassy car. You should think about becoming an ambassador."

His shoulders shake as he tries not to wake up my mom. "Sure. I'll get right on that."

ya and I discover that the Garden City Daffodils are a tightly knit bunch of women ranging in age and varying by nationality. They have a handful of vacancies left by beloved members who returned to their home countries and I worry that getting on the team will be hard. Except tryouts go something like this: We kick the ball around to warm up, we play a short scrimmage, and then we are welcomed onto the team by Karin, the Australian cofounder, and Jessica, the American.

Karin is in her early thirties with streaky blond hair, tanned skin, strong thighs, and a voice that carries. She serves as both the coach and the number one goalkeeper, and getting the ball past her proves really tough. I manage to score on her only once.

"We've never had a winning season and I wish we were more competitive," she admits. "But never to the exclusion of fun or to the point where we'd turn up our noses at new blood. If you're willing to be here, we're happy to have you."

She introduces us to the whole team. Too many to remember all at once, but Maude is a fifty-eight-year-old Brit who proudly proclaims herself the oldest player on the team. And Diya is a bank teller/midfielder who wears a hijab during practices and games. Aya loses her mind with excitement over this. Mathilde is French-Algerian. Sophie is from Ghana.

"I have never met so many people from so many different countries," Aya gushes. "I am probably not the best player, but I am very glad to be here."

It is really cool that all of these women have come to Cairo and found a way to make it feel like home, to create their own little clan. I am happy to meet them and even more happy to be back on a soccer field.

"I'm hoping to make the team at the American school in September," I explain to the group. "But if that happens, I wouldn't mind playing for two teams."

"You seem comfortable at forward," Jessica says, tightening her light brown ponytail as we take the field for drills. "Is that where you like to play?"

"Ideally, but I can play midfield, too. Whatever you need."

"We lost our scoring forward when she graduated from college. We can use the strength up front."

"I can't promise goals."

Jessica smiles and aims her thumb at Karin. "You got past her once. That's a good start."

"So I have to ask . . . what's up with the Daffodils?"

Karin's face dimples as she shakes her head. Clearly this is a question she's gotten before. "Since we're based in Garden City, we wanted a name that reflected that. I suggested we call ourselves Nightshade because it's deadly, you know?"

"That would make sense."

"Exactly, but Jess decided that because daffodil bulbs are poisonous, the flower is both beautiful and deadly. Great in concept. Not so much in execution because most people just think our name is cute."

"But we know the truth," Jessica insists. "That's all that matters."

Karin's indulgent smile makes it clear that their friendship is more important than the name of the team. "Okay," Karin says. "Let's get to work."

She puts us through some agility drills, and before the two-hour practice is over, we run another scrimmage. She positions me at right forward and Aya on the bench.

"Don't read anything into it," Karin assures her as we gather up our gear bags after practice. "I'll do a lot of shuffling around until I find the best combination. And you *will* play."

"I have never been a member of a team before," Aya says. "So it doesn't matter if I play only a little or not at all."

"Practices are Monday, Wednesday, and Thursday." Jessica hands us a printed sheet of all the players' names and phone numbers. "Games are on Sunday evenings when most of the Christian religious services are over and the sun is low. Hope to see you next time."

A dark-haired toddler runs to Karin and hugs her legs. She scoops him up and as she blows raspberries on his chubby cheek, her whole demeanor softens. He giggles and she leans forward to kiss a man who has the same dark hair as the little boy.

"This is my husband, Mohammed," she introduces. "And our son, Isaac. Caroline and Aya are new players and I have high hopes we might actually win a game with Caroline as striker."

"That's high praise," Mohammed says, his accent an adorable mix of Australian and Arabic. "Good luck to you, Caroline. Nice to meet you, Aya." He takes Isaac from her. "I'll meet you at the car, love."

"Is he, um—is he Muslim?" I ask.

"Yeah," Karin says. "Originally from Jordan."

"How . . . ?" I trail off, leaving the question unfinished. It's too forward to ask her if she converted to Islam for him. Or how they make their relationship work.

"I'm not easily offended," she says. "So if you've got a question, get on with it."

"Has it been hard?"

Karin's laugh rings out. "It's been a bloody nightmare. Mo's mother spent the better part of his life laying the foundation for an arranged marriage to the daughter of one of their neighbors. Then he came home from college with a blond, agnostic, big-mouth Australian wife, and to say it didn't go over well would be an understatement."

"Did she get over it?"

"Well, it helps that I've converted," she says. "So now she tolerates me. Fortunately, we only visit Jordan once a year. The rest of the time we are blissfully happy and trying for baby number two, which is too much information, isn't it?"

"A little, but that's okay. Did you, um—did you convert for him?"

"Actually, my husband encouraged me to study and decide if Islam was for me. Some of my extended family members back home think he forced the conversion, but Mo said I should want it for myself. Not for him."

I try to imagine myself in Karin's place, married to a Muslim (okay, I picture Adam), living in Cairo for the rest of my life. Converting to Islam. That's the hardest piece to envision. Catholicism has been a part of my life since baptism. I struggle to wake up on Sunday mornings for Mass, but once we're at church, I don't mind being there. I like listening to the Scripture readings. I like the off-key way our parish priest performs the singing parts. I like what I believe and can't see myself ever giving that up.

"I'm guessing you've got yourself an Egyptian boyfriend then?" Karin says.

"No. I mean, not really."

She laughs. "It's a yes-or-no question."

"It's complicated."

Karin slings her bag over her shoulder and pats mine. "Welcome to real life."

Dad goes back to the States again and real life moves on. I go down to the street each morning to buy bread, exchanging salaams and piastres with the bread seller. Mr. Elhadad drives Aya and me to soccer practice.

My parents put the kibosh on the trip to Hurghada, so instead Vivian and I create a game called "Elhadad Says" in which we ask Mr. Elhadad to drop us off somewhere in the city he thinks will be interesting. On our first day out, he takes us to Cairo Tower for a panoramic view of the entire city at 614 feet. The next time he takes us to the Egyptian Museum, where we overdose on pharaonic mummies.

I teach Stevie G. to sit in my hand and let me stroke his

belly. I send Hannah's box with the hieroglyph bracelet and a postcard filled with *X*s and *O*s but get an e-mail in return telling me she's been so busy with work and Vlad that she didn't have time to send a box for me.

I try not to think about Adam, but he is always somewhere in my head.

It's a Monday afternoon when I go downstairs to Mr. Elhadad's car and find Aya sitting in the passenger's seat—and Adam behind the wheel.

"Surprise!" she shouts.

"What's going on here?" I get in the backseat and close the door because nosy Masoud is watching. Adam looks at me in the rearview mirror with such longing that I want to wrap him in the fiercest hug and never let go. "Where's your dad?"

"I convinced him to let Adam drive me to practice," Aya says, her smile huge and proud. "I told him you were at Vivian's house and would be meeting us at the soccer field."

"You lied?"

"It had to be done," she insists. "My brother's unhappiness makes me sad. He misses cooking and he misses you. At a wedding in Helwan last week, the aunties were conspiring to match him with an Egyptian girl."

My heart constricts at the thought of Adam with someone who is not me. "Were they, um—did they succeed?"

He looks relieved as he shakes his head. "No."

"The two of you must be together," Aya says.

I love her dedication to romance, but I also know how difficult this is for her brother. As happy I am to see him, I don't want to get my hopes up.

"I cannot sneak around like Magdi," he says.

She shrugs. "Don't sneak. Just decide being together is more important than anyone who says you can't be happy— even if it is our parents who are saying it."

"It's not that simple," I say.

"Karin and Mohammed have done it. She said they are blissful."

"They're *married*."

"True," she says. "Your timing is too soon, but that does not mean you cannot be together. Fight for her, Adam."

"Would you be able to do this?" he asks finally. "To tell our mother that love is more important than her opinion and that you do not care what she thinks?"

Aya slumps back in her seat. "No."

I look out the window at a blurry Cairo as we drive silently to the soccer field, wishing we lived in a world where religions didn't matter and being with the person you love was easy. At practice I am distracted by his presence, until Karin comes over. "What the hell is wrong with you today?"

"He's here. Sitting over on the stands, watching me suck."

"Then stop sucking. This"—she gestures at the field, at the women around us—"has nothing to do with him. This realm belongs to you." Karin touches the center of my forehead. "If you can't put him out of your mind, at least show him that in your realm you are the queen."

Laughing, I wipe my nose on my sleeve. "Okay. Let's do this."

She benches me as we start scrimmaging, and as I stand on the sidelines, I do some juggling tricks with my feet and knees. Total showboat moves. When I look over at the metal bleachers, Adam's attention is on me. I throw a smile over my shoulder, then do a rainbow flick, a move that sends the ball back, up, and over my head. It lands on the ground in front of me. It's a trick that's taken me years to perfect, but the payoff is worth it. Adam is smiling as he shakes his head.

"Caroline, you're up," Sophie says as she jogs to the sidelines.

I run onto the field and spend the next ten minutes playing as hard as I can, scoring on Karin. I do a cartwheel and she puts both hands up for high fives. "The queen."

When practice is over, Adam comes down to the field. I kick the ball in his direction and he stops it with his foot, pinning it to the ground as I approach. I'm not sure what to say now that we have a chance to talk. "I named my lovebird Stevie G."

His shoulders quake as he laughs at how I named my bird after Liverpool's former captain. "Hopefully he will be worthy of the name."

"He lets me hold him without biting."

"Give him time and I am certain he will love you." Adam rolls the ball back to me. I trap it with my foot.

"How's your new job?"

"Waiting tables is not so bad, but it's very difficult to be so near the kitchen in a fine hotel and not be cooking."

"I'm sorry."

"I want to believe this is not my final fate. But sometimes I fear I will spend my life standing beside what I desire and not be allowed to have it," he says. "Geddo called it a dreaming disease and said I should gratefully accept whatever Allah gives me, but I cannot turn off my dreams. It is like asking me not to breathe."

"Your dreams will happen, Adam," I say, but the only thing I have any certainty about is my faith in him. His reality may never live up to his expectations, even with both of us rooting him on.

He reaches out as if he's going to touch me, then drops his hand away. "You are better at football than I imagined. And in my imagination, you are always better than me."

I kick the ball to him. "Show me."

He rolls it back and forth beneath his shoe, hesitating. I sweep out with my left foot, taking it from him and running toward the goal. Adam gives chase—I can hear his footsteps pounding in the grass behind me—and comes up level, but when he tries to steal the ball, I step over it, protecting it, and keep moving forward. As we close in on the goal, Adam runs forward to guard the net. I launch the ball. He dives to block. He misses.

He laughs from down there on the ground. "It is a very good thing my esteem is not tied to my ability to play football."

I help him to stand and there, in front of the team, in front of his sister, I kiss him. My hands on his face. My hands in his hair. My toes skim the ground as he lifts me nearly off my feet, kissing me back.

"Next year I'll go home and someday you'll marry someone else," I say. "If I'm only meant to be a footnote in the history of Adam Elhadad, then maybe we should make it a really good footnote."

He strokes my cheek with his thumb. "I have tried to put you out of my mind, but you are always there."

Despite having known each other most of our lives, Owen and I took a long time to use the word "love." Adam and I could be mistaking what we feel for something else. Except my parents eloped after knowing each other for only a month and they're still together. Maybe it's possible that what Adam and I have is real.

I rest my forehead against his. *"Bahebik."*

"Caroline." He bites his lower lip, trying to keep a smile from overtaking his face. "To me you would say *bahebak*."

"Save the language lesson for another day, Elhadad. I love you, too."

CHAPTER 29

*W*hoa. What?" Hannah says after I fill her in on everything that has gone down since the last time we had a video chat. "Why didn't you tell me any of this?"

"You were busy with Vlad."

"The bracelet is so beautiful, by the way." She holds up her wrist so I can see it. "Thank you. And I'm sorry I've been such a crappy friend."

"It's okay. I've been busy too."

"Obviously."

I laugh. "I meant that I'm playing on a soccer team with Aya and hanging out with Vivian, a girl from my new school. Oh, and I almost forgot! Adam bought me a lovebird that I've been training to do tricks. Hang on."

I bring Stevie G. out of his cage and Hannah squeals when she sees him. The bird climbs from my hand up to my shoulder, where he plays with my earring and chatters softly in my ear.

"So what happened with Adam's family?" Hannah asks.

"They attempted another family intervention, but Adam basically told them he'd be making his own decisions about his relationship from now on, which—well, match meet gasoline. His uncle blamed Adam's dad, saying that if Mr. Elhadad wasn't so obsessed with westerners his children wouldn't be behaving like them. And now every time I'm in the car with him, I feel like he's up there in the front seat thinking about how I've corrupted his son. Mr. Elhadad used to be kind of . . . fatherly . . . and now he's not. And Adam's mother feels pretty disrespected. My mom invited the family for dinner, hoping maybe we could talk through the whole mess, and Mrs. Elhadad said no."

"Seems like it would be easier not to date Adam."

"Sure. Break up with Vlad and tell me how easy it is."

Hannah's eyes go wide. "Wow. You *really* like him."

"I really do."

"What about when you come home?"

"Remember how you said you were trying not to think about the end of the summer? It's like that."

"Then I probably shouldn't tell you this, but . . . Vlad is staying in the United States," Hannah says. "He's going to graduate school at the University of Michigan, so with me at Toledo . . ."

"I officially hate you."

Hannah's laugh fades to a thoughtful silence. "Things have changed so much," she says. "New friends. New boyfriends. Sometimes I worry you'll come home and I won't know you anymore."

"I worry you're going to forget about me."

"I'm really sorry about the box."

"It might be hard to sustain anyway," I say. "But you aren't allowed to bail on our next chat. And as much as I like him, no Vlad."

She holds up three Girl Scout fingers. "I promise."

"Love you to the moon," I say.

Hannah blows me a kiss with those same three fingers. "And back."

CHAPTER 30

My mother is angry," Adam says when we talk about his family. He calls from his bedroom and the sound of his voice in my ear is a new intimacy. "She is against me having a girlfriend, especially one who is not Muslim, and she thinks you will change me into someone who is unsatisfied with the gifts Allah has given me. She thinks you make me want things that are not meant for a poor Egyptian boy."

My memory casts back to our first day in Cairo when Mom accused Dad of giving Adam too much money, of raising his expectations to an unreachable level. "My mom worries about the same thing. She's afraid I'll break your heart."

"You will," he says. "But I am not afraid."

The next new intimacy is on his next day off work, when

Adam comes over to the apartment just to hang out. It feels good to sit close together on the couch, watching Liverpool highlight videos from games past. We take Stevie G. out of his cage and watch him chase his plastic ball around the living room floor. And having a boyfriend who cooks pays off in a big way at lunchtime, when Adam makes hummus grilled cheese sandwiches with feta and sliced olives. We eat them on the balcony as feluccas sail past on the river. As easy as it could be to get carried away, we keep our hormones in check. But it is nice to be able to kiss each other without worrying who might be watching. We kiss a *lot*.

We don't see each other as frequently as we did when he was my stand-in driver—Adam works long hours and spends time trying to repair his relationship with his family—but we go to the movies, sometimes in English, sometimes in Arabic. I ask him not to translate the Arabic movies so I can figure out on my own what's happening, and he laughs when I get the plot completely wrong. I don't tell him that sometimes I get the plot wrong on purpose, just to make him smile.

We see concerts at the Culture Wheel with his friends. Bahar doesn't always show up, but when he does, he doesn't acknowledge me. I am sad on Adam's behalf that their friendship is broken, but I don't know how to fix it. Other times we hang out with my American friends and I have to remind them to slow down when they're talking so Adam can keep up with the conversation. Once, he comes for dinner with my mom and me at our apartment. But my favorite thing is being alone with him, driving up to Mokattam, where we talk. Kiss. Dream.

September arrives with my dad's return from the tugboat. Summer is almost over and school will start soon. Mom is at the clinic the day he gets back and our kitchen is in total disarray as Adam sets out to prove to me that his *koshary* is better than the recipe served at his old restaurant.

"What's going on in here?" Dad asks, surveying the tower of pots in the sink.

"Well, sometimes when a boy and girl are alone together . . . ," I say. "They make *koshary*."

He laughs as he kisses my forehead and pats Adam on the back. Dad's caught in a weird middle place because he's the only parent who keeps his concerns to himself. He says the consequences of my relationship with Adam—regardless of the outcome—are part of growing up and we're just going to have to deal with them. "Nice to see you, kid."

My dad unpacks his duffel and takes a short nap, and then we put Adam's claim to the test. It takes a special ability to know what a dish needs without seeing it marked down in cups and tablespoons, but Adam possesses that ability. I can't say what makes his *koshary* better than the restaurant's—as most of the ingredients are the same—but there is something more refined about it. Like it belongs on a plate instead of scooped into a margarine tub. Like this boy is destined for greatness. (Maybe I'm biased.)

"We've been thinking about taking the train to Alexandria for a day," I tell Dad as we eat. "It's only a couple of hours away and the fare is supercheap. Would that be okay?"

"Have you asked your mom?"

"Not yet."

"We'll need to talk before I answer this question," he says. "When you went to Fayoum you had guides responsible for you, so I'm not completely cool with this going-alone plan. I'd worry about both of you."

"You could come with us and, you know, pay for everything."

Dad chuckles. "Now I see what you're really after."

"We could dive on Cleopatra's palace." I know as I say it that I'm pushing one of his buttons. Scuba diving is one of my dad's favorite things that he doesn't get to do very often. The last time we went was two years ago in the Florida Keys.

"Count me in," Dad says. "We'll go tomorrow."

"I thought you needed to talk to Mom."

"I'll convince her."

When my mom gets home from work, she rubber-stamps

the trip only if Dad goes with us. "Just be supercareful," she says, then eyes my dad. "Including you."

"Come with us," he says.

But Mom begs off. "I've got a summer cold brewing and a cataract surgery first thing in the morning. I'm going to overdose on vitamin C tonight, get some extra sleep, and hope I'm feeling better in the morning."

The atmosphere in the car feels heavy and the radio is silent as Mr. Elhadad drives us to Ramses Station. He speaks in quiet Arabic to Adam, who responds in kind. I don't understand what they are saying, but I look out the window to give them privacy anyway.

"Be sure to buy tickets for the special," Mr. Elhadad says to my dad when we reach the station. "It is a nonstop express with comfortable seats and air-conditioning. Much nicer. More tourists, fewer Egyptians."

Adam says something to his father and Mr. Elhadad pulls him in for a hug. He pats his son's shoulder before getting back into the car.

"Are you okay?" I ask as my dad pays for the tickets. Adam looks a little dazed.

"I have spent my entire life in Cairo," he says as we walk down the platform to the train. "But in three hours I will be in

Alexandria, the farthest from my home I have ever been, and I will swim in the sea."

"Are you nervous?"

"Yes," he says. "My family worries you are taking me to a place from where I cannot return."

The platforms are busy with people waiting to board trains that look ancient, trains that are run-down by use. The special train is painted in the colors of the Egyptian flag—red on top, white in the middle, black on the bottom—and looks newer. Not all that different from Amtrak's Lake Shore Limited train that runs past Sandusky every day.

"Is it possible that you're not meant to return?" I say as I choose a seat beside the window. Adam sits next to me with my dad across the aisle.

"What do you mean?" Adam asks.

"My grandparents have lived in the same town all their lives and they are completely content with that choice," I say. "And that's fine, you know? But not everyone is meant to stay in one place. Maybe Alexandria is just your first step."

"Perhaps." He toys with his lower lip as he considers and I wonder if I'm projecting my vision of his future onto him. It could be that he wants to stay in Cairo, with his family. That he's happy right where he is.

"I've never ridden in a proper train before." I wiggle a little in my seat, changing the subject and making him laugh a little. "I feel like I'm on my way to Hogwarts."

"In which house will you be sorted when we arrive?"

"You know about Harry Potter?" I ask, and his eyebrows hitch up, as if he can't believe I'm asking this question. After the whole reggae band thing, I should probably know better. "Sorry."

"My mother has a cousin who lives in America. He sent the first book to Aya and me, and my father read it aloud, translating to Arabic. When he finished, he bought the second book in English and said if we wanted to read it, we must learn to read it ourselves."

"Is that the real reason your English is so good?"

"The books were very good motivation for me," he admits. "Harry Potter was yet another thing that made Geddo angry because Islam considers magic to be blasphemous."

"A lot of Christians get twisted about the magic, too."

"My parents did not let us go blindly into that world," Adam says. "We read the books together and talked about what was false and what was true. But as far as Geddo was concerned, the only book Muslims should read is the Quran."

"So which house are you in?"

"No. No. I asked you first."

"Hufflepuff."

"Of course." He laughs. "Same."

"Really?"

"I shared the book with my friends," Adam says. "Magdi's parents paid no attention and Omar read the books in secret. Afterward, we took the sorting quiz and they teased me without mercy about being a Hufflepuff."

"Did Bahar ever read the books?"

"He refused because his parents forbid it."

"It's too bad," I say. "You could have used another Hufflepuff in your corner."

Adam laughs. "This is true."

There are too many people around, including my dad, for me to kiss him, but I give his hand a squeeze. "Trade seats with me."

"Why?"

"If we're going somewhere you've never been, you should see it."

"You have never been to Alexandria," Adam says.

"I know, but I can see it on the way back."

"You make no sense, but I *would* like to look out the window."

We swap places. He puts his arm around me and I lean into him for most of the ride, so I can see out the window too. Once we are out of the tightly packed Cairo skyline, the railway runs along the Nile where the land around us is green.

Scrawny cows dot the riverbank and men in little skiffs fish the water. We pass ramshackle villages and farmlands, all pushed up against their liquid power cord. As we near Alexandria, urban sprawl seeps back into the landscape until we are in the heart of the city.

CHAPTER 31

We take a taxi from the train station to the diving center, a small waterfront complex that is reminiscent of those found in the Florida Keys. The shop sits beside a tiki-hut restaurant, and their jetty is lined with dive boats and inflatable dinghies. The day is clear so both the sky and the Mediterranean Sea are intensely blue, and the circular harbor is filled with boats of all sizes. Some are moored while others kick up small white wakes as they move across the water.

Dad books a day trip and our team is the dive master Ramy and his assistant Khalid. Ramy outfits us with gear and takes us to a small pool where he instructs Adam on how to use the scuba equipment. My dad and I have official dive certification, but Ramy puts Adam through an introductory course that will allow him to dive without certification.

"Cleopatra's palace is in about five meters of water," Ramy says. "Good for a beginner since it's not very deep. You won't need to decompress on the way up, so if you feel uncomfortable for any reason, swim to the surface."

As we motor out toward the dive site, the beaches rimming the harbor are thick with people and beach umbrellas. A few white tourists are wearing bikinis, but most Egyptian women walk fully clothed along the shoreline. A couple women wearing abayas and hijabs are farther out in the water.

I opted for a long-sleeve rash guard and boy-short bottoms, but my choice of swimwear is less distracting to Adam than his state of shirtlessness is to me. I keep stealing glances at the light dusting of dark hair in the middle of his chest and the definition of his back muscles, and I'm thankful I'm wearing sunglasses.

"The visibility here isn't as good as Sharm El Sheikh or Hurghada because the water is shallow and choppy," Khalid explains. "But I think today won't be so bad. Many of the intact artifacts were removed to museum collections, but you will see some granite pillars, food storage bowls, and two of the sphinxes that guarded Cleopatra's temple."

The dive site isn't very far from shore, not even as far as the middle of the harbor. As Khalid ties the boat off to a mooring ball, Ramy points out the spot where the lighthouse of Alexandria once stood. Although the lighthouse is long gone, it's still kind of exciting that I've visited two of the Seven Wonders of the Ancient World. Infinitely better than staying home in Ohio with my grandparents.

Dad and I start putting on our gear, but Adam just sits in the boat looking a little dazed. "Is this too much?" I ask. "We could snorkel or just swim."

"No." He looks back at Alexandria, then smiles at me. "I'm fine. I'm ready."

Khalid remains on the boat while Ramy takes the rest of us into the water. We make a human chain, holding each other's hands as we descend, because the water is kind of murky. As we near the bottom, dark shapes begin taking form. Unlike in Florida, there is no elaborate coral growth and only a few colorful fish, but the sea floor is littered with square and cylindrical segments of the pillars that once supported Cleopatra's palace. Everything is crusted with barnacles, but Ramy points out a number of large stone bowls and Dad swims through a tunnel formed by large blocks of rubble. We follow our dive master—and a school of tiny silver fish—to the body of a sphinx about the size of a horse. The head is missing but the shape is intact. Not far away is a second sphinx, this one barnacle-free to get a better idea of what it originally looked like, but again headless. I wonder if the heads were stolen and make a note to ask when we surface. We stay down for about an hour and even though pillars make up most of what we see, it is clear that the palace complex was huge. Fit for the queen of Egypt.

Finally, Ramy taps his watch, signaling that our time is up, and we swim to the surface.

Adam yanks the regulator from his mouth, and his face is nothing but smile.

"This was the most exciting thing I have ever done," he says. "I had difficulty not shouting bubbles at everything we saw."

"You should see the reefs down in the—"

"Your phones have been going crazy," Khalid interrupts from up in the boat. "Many text messages and missed calls, I think. I did not read them, but someone is trying desperately to reach you."

We scramble into the boat and Dad grabs his cell phone with wet hands. A stricken look crosses his face as he listens to his voice mail. "Shit," he says. "We need to leave. *Now.*"

"Dad, what's wrong?"

Adam's phone and mine are both filled with messages from my mother saying **Call me right away** and **I am okay, but call me ASAP.**

The dive team quickly unties the boat, and Ramy drives us back toward Alexandria as my dad phones Mom.

"Beck, are you hurt? Where are you?" he says, and my hands

start to shake. What is happening? Adam takes my hand, but he looks worried too. "We're on our way . . . no, I'll rent a car . . . we'll be there as fast as we can . . . I love you, too . . . I'll be there soon."

"Dad?"

"A car bomb exploded outside the clinic." His tanned skin has gone pale. "She wasn't there."

"Oh, thank God," I say at the same time Adam, Ramy, and Khalid all say, *"Alhamdulillah."*

"She was feeling worse this morning when we left," Dad says. "So Jamie went to the clinic in her place. He was killed in the blast, along with two patients. Your mom is blaming herself. So we need to get back fast."

"The distance to Cairo is the same by car or train," Adam says.

"Yeah, but the train doesn't leave until this afternoon," my dad points out. "We don't have that kind of time."

"I will have to drive."

If this were any other situation, I would laugh. But just like on the day of Mr. Elhadad's heart attack, Adam's utter fearlessness behind the wheel might be exactly what we need right now.

We reach the jetty and Dad jumps out of the boat. Khalid follows. "I will take you to the car rental."

Twenty minutes later, outside the rental agency, Dad thanks him and offers him baksheesh for everything he's done. Khalid pushes it away. "I hope your wife will be okay."

"Thank you," Dad says. "I hope so too."

We are a damp mess as we enter the rental agency, but Adam takes over, laying out the situation in Arabic. Dad signs the paperwork and offers up his credit card, but once the car is pulled around to the front of the building and we have the keys, Adam takes the wheel. I use the GPS on my phone to guide us out of Alexandria, and once we are on the highway, Adam's foot rests heavy on the accelerator. In the backseat, Dad calls Mom again.

"We're on our way," he says. "Adam is driving . . . aw, Beck, don't . . . you're not a terrible human being for laughing at the kid's driving skills . . ."

Dad stays on the phone with her the entire way back to Cairo, talking softly, telling her comforting stories she already knows about when they met, reassuring her that he'll be there soon. One thing he never says is that everything will be okay, which worries me, because *will* everything be okay? He flings open the car door before the car stops in front of the apartment building and runs toward the vestibule.

"Go to your mother," Adam says. "I will take care of the car."

I sprint after my dad, up the stairs, and arrive at the apartment just behind him, just as Mom launches herself from the couch and he catches her in his arms. She sobs into his shoulder and the sound is one I have never heard. My mom is always strong. She rarely cries. To see her so broken brings tears to my own eyes. Through the blur I see Mrs. Elhadad rise from the couch.

"I will go now," she says quietly to me.

"Thank you for being here." I step forward and she lets me hug her. The soft pat of her hand on my back is comforting.

"If you need something," Mrs. Elhadad says, "please say."

Nodding, I thank her once more. She looks to the door when Adam comes in and speaks softly to him in Arabic. He glances at me as he follows his mother out the door, his eyes filled with questions and concerns.

"You and your crazy driving came through again," I call after him. "Thank you."

I want to ask my mom what happens next. Will OneVision send us home? Or open a new clinic in a different part of the city? What if whoever was responsible for the bombing wants to try again? What if Mom isn't so lucky the second time? My breath catches in my chest. Even though she wasn't killed today, she could have been. People who were alive this morning are dead now. They were *loved* and now they are *gone*. But I can't ask her anything because Dad leads her into the bedroom and closes the door.

CHAPTER 32

*Y*esterday morning, according to witnesses in Manshiyat Nasr, a car pulled to the curb alongside the clinic. A man wearing an ordinary blue button-up shirt and jeans got out and walked away. Just a little more than a minute later, the car erupted into a giant ball of fire and the ground convulsed like an earthquake. Windows in the bakery across the street shattered. Stucco and brick spewed out in every direction. And when the fireball subsided, the car was nothing but a burning frame and the clinic was a pile of rubble.

"I was still asleep." Mom's eyes are still puffy and pink from crying, even after eleven hours of sleep. She leans against Dad as they sit on the couch like he's the only thing holding her up right now. He might be. "Safa, our office assistant, woke me up to say she was running late, then called back to tell me the clinic was just . . . gone."

Tears well up in her eyes and she pauses, takes a deep breath and a small sip of coffee. "I threw on some clothes and went to Manshiyat Nasr, but the police would not let me inside the cordon, even after I showed them my OneVision identification."

She tells us that she didn't want to sit at home doing nothing, so she stayed at the scene and treated people who had been injured in the blast—shrapnel injuries, mostly, from glass and brick—until a police commander agreed to speak with her.

"He confirmed that three bodies had been found in the rubble but had not yet been identified," she says. "I called Jamie's phone over and over. Then I called Sarah, who told me he'd forgotten his lunch when he left for work. If he had just gone back—"

Mom's face crumples and she breaks down again, crying into Dad's shoulder. He strokes her hair and I struggle with my own tears. How can someone justify blowing up innocent people? How can anyone believe that is what God wants?

"He—he had his whole career ahead of him." She blows her nose and blinks rapidly as she continues. "If I had been there—Casey, it should have been me."

"Hey." Dad touches her chin and she looks up at him. "There was no scenario yesterday that would have left the world a better place today. If you'd been there, I'd have lost my wife and Caroline would have lost her mother, but someone would still be dead. I get that it's hard not to blame yourself, Beck, but none of this is your fault."

"When I spoke with the regional director from OneVision, he reminded me that everyone knows the risks when they agree to the job," Mom says. "But I was supposed to do that surgery. I was supposed to be there."

"You're not Wonder Woman."

"I have a *cold*, Casey," she says. "If I had just sucked it up and gone to work—"

"Do they know who did it?" I interrupt, trying to derail her guilt. "Was it ISIS?"

"No, but it was a young sympathizer who wanted to impress the Islamic State by targeting a foreign-run clinic in a predominantly Christian neighborhood," she says. "He bragged about it on Twitter and was reported to the police by one of his own friends."

Dad finally asks the question that's been on my mind since yesterday. "So what happens now, Beck?"

"OneVision believes this was an isolated incident, but they have to decide if they are going to continue operating in Cairo or relocate."

"What do *you* want to do?"

Mom sighs. "I don't know. Part of me wants to turn tail and run, but that's not who I am. I made a commitment."

"Don't forget about the commitment you made to me," my dad says. "When I said till death do us part, I didn't think you meant to put yourself directly in its path."

The corner of her mouth trembles a little, like she can't decide whether to laugh or cry. She does both as she rests her head on his shoulder. "I know."

He kisses her hair. "I need you, Beck. Maybe it's time to go home."

Mom goes back to bed and Dad sits on the balcony making calls. We don't know if the bombing made the national news back in the States, so he fills in the details to my grandparents and Uncle Mike. I can only imagine the "I told you so" from Grandma Irene. I go to my room, where I find a text on my phone from Adam: **How is your mother?**

She feels responsible for her coworker's death and guilty that she is alive.

I'm sorry, he writes. Then, **Teta has been cooking all day. She would like to bring food for your family. Would that be okay?**

I go out onto the balcony and walk quietly past my parents' bedroom to where my dad is sitting. "Adam's grandma wants to bring over some food."

"I haven't even thought about dinner," he says. "That would be welcome."

Yes, I text back to Adam. **Please.**

* * *

All five members of the Elhadad family turn up at our apartment, and any disapproval, any anger, is hidden beneath an avalanche of food. Adam's grandmother, laden with shopping bags filled with plastic containers, disappears into the kitchen. Mom gets out of bed and brushes her teeth. If this were a proper visit, we would offer an appetizer, but today the world is upside down and our guests have brought their own baba ghanoush.

Mrs. Elhadad wraps her arms tightly around my mom, who dissolves into tears again. Adam's mother touches her forehead to Mom's and the two women stand this way, with Mrs. Elhadad speaking softly in Arabic, until my mother pulls back, nodding, and wipes her tears. Whatever transpired between them was private, but as the two women settle on the couch, Mom looks lighter somehow. Her smile, though fragile, is still a smile.

The elder Mrs. Elhadad comes from the kitchen with food and drinks. While the adults talk about the bombing, Adam, Aya, and I take our sodas into my bedroom. I leave the door open.

"Will you have to go home?" Aya asks as she looks at the photo of Hannah and Owen. For all the time we've spent playing soccer together, this is the first time she's been to my apartment.

"I hope not," I say. "Three months ago I didn't even want

to come here, but now I want to keep playing soccer with the Daffodils and school starts next week."

The thought of leaving is painful, but I know going home isn't the worst thing that could happen. The worst has already happened.

"Do you guys want to go for a walk?" I ask.

Dad and Mr. Elhadad give their permission for us to go, provided we don't go far and we're back in half an hour. The bombing has rattled us all, as if danger knows where we live now, as if it followed us right to our front door. The three of us cross the road and walk down to the park. Once inside its leafy confines, Adam holds my hand. We haven't had a chance to talk since Alexandria. His excitement over scuba diving got lost in the shuffle and even now it feels improper to talk about happy things, but as a dinner cruise boat motors past, Adam takes the leash off his enthusiasm.

"It was as if the world had suddenly doubled in size," he says. "And it felt like touching history. I can't . . . I have no words to explain it."

"Were you frightened?" Aya asks.

"Only at first."

She offers him a reluctant smile. "You are like a cork that has been freed from the neck of a bottle. I worry that you have grown too large to fit back in the bottle."

"You sound like Ummi."

"Do you think our mother's concerns are not valid?"

"No," Adam says. "Which is the reason I am going to speak with her and Baba about attending culinary school. I do not want to go back into the bottle."

His sister's dark eyes go wide for a moment, and then her dimples appear. "Very good. I was afraid you were willing to accept being a waiter at the Ritz-Carlton. I'm happy you have a plan."

I lift myself on tiptoe and kiss his cheek. "I'm proud of you."

Adam slips his arm around my waist and presses his lips to my temple. "I hope your family will stay in Egypt."

"Me too."

When we return to the apartment, the dining room table is spread with bowls of lamb stew, small stuffed zucchini, pickled onions, and tomato salad. We take our places around the table; despite the circumstances, this meal is less awkward than our last together. The line between guest and host has blurred, and all of us are united in the goal of helping Mom feel better. She looks less stressed and Adam's grandma seems genuinely happy to provide comfort by way of enough food to feed a small army.

Even after the meal has been cleared away and the leftovers stowed in the refrigerator, we sit around the table until late into the night. At some point, both my mom and Mrs. Elhadad moved closer to their husbands. Dad's arm is stretched along the back of Mom's chair, and Mr. Elhadad holds his wife's hand.

"How did you get together?" my dad asks.

Mrs. Elhadad explains that they were introduced through family members. "It was not a forced marriage," she says. "Both of us could say no, but I met Ahmed and—"

"She could not resist me." Mr. Elhadad is joking, but the way she smiles at him makes it clear that it's not really a joke. She does the same little shrug-nod combination as I've seen Adam do, and it's kind of adorable. "It was the same for him."

Mr. Elhadad laughs. "True."

"I was a deckhand when Beck and I met," Dad says. "I was living at home in the Bronx with my folks and she was going to medical school at Fordham. We saw each other in a club one night, she let me buy her a drink, and we got married about a month later."

Adam's eyes meet mine across the table and my cheeks flame. Our parents are proof that love can happen fast. Maybe Adam and I are proof, too. But our parents lived in the same city. Shared the same faith. And were old enough to make a real commitment to each other. How can our relationship last if I have to go home? Six thousand miles is so far.

I stand and collect the stray dessert plates, needing to get away for a few minutes. As I'm loading the dishwasher, Dad comes into the kitchen. "It's not like you to voluntarily do the dishes. What's up, Bug?"

"Nothing."

"Sure?"

"Yeah. I'm just tired."

"It's been a long few days," he says. "Leave this be and go to bed."

Adam's grandma comes into the kitchen and starts gathering her plastic storage containers. I mime an offer to wash them before they leave, but she waves me off. Back in the dining room, Mr. Elhadad finishes the dregs of his coffee. "It is getting late," he says. "We should go."

"Thank you for the food and the company," Mom says, hugging both women and Aya. "I didn't know how much I needed this until you arrived."

"You are welcome," Mr. Elhadad says. "This we do for friends."

It is after midnight when the door finally closes behind them. I go to my room, and as I change into my pajamas, I receive a text from Adam.

I am not ready for good-bye.

CHAPTER 33

*O*ur time in Cairo ends the same way it began: in an empty apartment surrounded by cardboard with Adam Elhadad helping us.

OneVision decided not to open another clinic in Cairo—at least not this year—and gave my mother the option of working in either Haiti or Malawi. After a quick week in Ohio, Mom will fly to Port-au-Prince and then take a bus to her new clinic. Because she'll be bunking with other aid workers in a hurricane-devastated area of the island, Dad and I will live with Grandma Jim and Grandma Rose until the lease runs out on our house. I'll start my senior year with Hannah and Owen. Like I never left.

Our furniture is like new, no worn spots on the chairs or accidental drink rings on the coffee table. It still even smells a little bit like IKEA. Adam's dad will sell the furniture for us, but we box up everything we can't carry in our suitcases, including all the decorative items from the markets. I decide to leave Stevie G. with Aya because birds imported into the United States must be quarantined for a month—too long for a little lovebird accustomed to getting lots of love.

I pick up the Kelleys Island stone from my nightstand. There has never been any question that Dad and I would go to the island one more time, but I thought it would happen after our year in Egypt.

"I want you to have this," I say to Adam. "To, um—I guess to remember me."

He tucks a strand of hair behind my ear and holds his fingertips against the side of my neck. "Do you think I will forget you?"

"You probably should."

"I won't."

"Is that all we'll ever be to each other? Memories?"

"I don't know how we can be anything else," he says. "Six thousand miles is a very long distance."

"I just—I hate the thought of living in the same world as you and not knowing you anymore."

Adam holds my face in his hands as he kisses me, slowly. Softly. Heat rushes through me, warming me to my toes. I slip my arms up around his neck, sinking my fingers into his hair as I catch his lower lip gently between mine. We press close, then closer. Kiss for days. Until our breathing is ragged and my lips come away feeling as if they are still being kissed.

His forehead is against mine as he says, "Staying in contact would feel the same as standing outside the kitchen door at the hotel and knowing what is on the other side is not for me."

"I don't want you to become a memory."

My eyes burn with tears as we make another go-round on this endless circle of wanting what we can't have.

"I always believed dating was haram because it could lead to sinful behavior," he says. "But now I think it's because you carry the other person with you forever. I have been changed by you."

"You made my world bigger."

"And you did the same for me."

"So what do we do?" I say. "Torture ourselves by following each other on Facebook? I mean, I want you to be happy, but I *really* don't want to see it when your mother finds you a wife."

"I think our only choice is to say good-bye."

A tear trickles down his face, and as he reaches up to wipe it away, I take his hand. I kiss his cheek, trapping the tear against my lips, and I think sadness tastes the same everywhere in the world. "I'm still going to love you."

"And I will love you."

My dad taps on the open door frame and I pull back, wiping my eyes with the sleeve of my shirt.

"I'm sorry to rush you," Dad says. "But we need to leave soon. Are you finished packing?"

My duffel bag looks bloated as it sits on the floor beside my empty desk, and my backpack might be too full to fit in the overhead compartment, but I nod. "Yeah."

Dad grabs the bags and takes them into the living room.

"Caroline," Mom calls. "There's someone here to see you."

Vivian stands in the path between boxes. She wraps me up in a tight hug. "I was so looking forward to hanging out with you at school this year," she says. "But I guess we're going to have to look for each other in New York next fall, right?"

I smile. "Right."

"I can't stay because my driver's got the car idling at the curb." Vivian releases me. "But stay in touch, okay?"

"Definitely. You too."

My friend is gone as quick as she came and then it's time for us to leave. There are so many things I'm going to miss about Cairo: the Nile right outside my bedroom window, buying fresh bread in the morning, the incessant noise, even the call to prayer. But mostly I am going to miss the people.

"We are sad to see you go," Mr. Elhadad says as we gather

up our bags. "I am sorry my country has driven you away."

"Egypt has given us far more reason to stay," Mom says. "And I'm sorry we have to leave."

"I count you as friends." He hugs Dad, Mom, and then me. We've come so far from the first day, when I didn't even know if I should shake his hand. "And I will hope a day will come when you return."

Mr. Elhadad stays behind to sort out what will be sold and what will be sent to us. He'll meet with the rental agent to give him our payment for breaking the lease. Dad also left Mr. Elhadad with an envelope containing enough money to cover the driver's fee for September, even though the month has only just started.

Adam drives us to the airport, rocketing through traffic, zipping in and out of spaces that seem too small for the car to fit, and making too-sharp turns. "You know, if cooking doesn't work out," I say, "you could always get a job as a stunt driver in Hollywood."

He laughs. "Only if I do not have to play the villain."

"Never," I say. "Always the hero."

The departure lanes are flooded with cars and taxis, but Adam manages to squeeze the car into a spot between a battered taxi and a shiny Mercedes. He takes our bags from the trunk, and when they are lined up in a neat row on the curb, it is time for the real good-bye. There are people all around us—just like when we arrived—and some of them might be staring at my beautiful mother or my tattooed dad, but my eyes are locked on Adam. My vision blurs as he shakes hands with Dad and accepts a hug from Mom. The tears spill over when Adam and I are as alone as we can be at a crowded airport, standing face-to-face.

"I want you to have the best life," I say. "Even if I'm not a part of it."

He kisses me good-bye in front of my parents, in front of everyone, his hands on my face and my fingers tangled in his hair. The moment is sweet and perfect and it obliterates my heart. He strokes my cheek one last time. *"Ma'a salama."*

"Good-bye."

I follow my parents through the sliding doors into the airport, which makes me shiver after living in the Cairo heat. I look back. Adam is leaning against the car—just like always—and I'm flooded with longing. To run back to him. To stay. He touches his hand to his chest and then walks around to the driver's door. I start to wave, but a random shoulder bumps against mine, forcing me to pay attention to where I am going. When I look back once more—through yet another haze of tears—Adam is gone.

CHAPTER 34

Memories of Cairo are never very far from my mind, especially in New York City, where a sound or a scent (or some random guy hitting on me as I walk to class) will send me back. I think about Adam Elhadad more than I should, too. My parents assumed I would get over him with time. Owen thought we could be a couple again, as if Egypt never happened. And sometimes—when I was playing soccer on my own team or sitting in class with my old friends— it felt as if Cairo was nothing more than a dream. But the catch in my chest whenever I remember Adam reminds me that he was real.

Today the sway of the N train transports me to a crowded ladies' car on the metro. Especially when, across the aisle, an elderly lady reads her Bible. I watch her for a few seconds, then look out the window at the October sky and smile to myself as the memories overtake me again.

The sky is bright blue and the air is crisp. Cool enough for a sweater but not so cold that I need my coat. I wear my favorite scarf—the red one with multicolored tassels—that I bought at the Friday Market. My new roommate, Maggie, thinks I'm an Egyptophile because my bed is draped with an Egyptian quilt, a tapestry hangs on my side of the room, and a star-shaped lantern decorates my desk along with a little stuffed camel. On move-in day, I told her I'd lived in Cairo for a few months last year. I like Maggie, but I don't know her well enough yet to admit I have all these things because they make me feel like I'm still there—a little bit, at least.

As the train passes over the East River, I glance down at the postcard in my hand. On the front is a sunset-over-the-pyramids scene with GREETINGS FROM CAIRO (my Arabic is slowly improving) written across the bottom. Super touristy, just like the rest of the postcards pinned to the bulletin board over my desk. The first one arrived about a month after I got back to Ohio. It was a picture from Khan el-Khalili and on the back it said: "If there is a way to stop myself from thinking about you, I have yet to discover it."

The soccer team captainship had gone to someone else, Hannah was still crazy in love with Vlad, and Owen wasn't really speaking to me. So I sent back a postcard with a picture of Lake Erie that said: "My life doesn't fit me anymore."

Every month since then we have traded postcards with single-line snapshots of our lives. From me: "Good-bye, Sandusky. Hello, Fordham." From him: "Finally I am on the other side of the kitchen door." On the back of this card is an Egyptian postage stamp and a New York City address with the message: "Go to my cousin's restaurant. There will be a gift there for you."

At the Astoria Boulevard station, I exit the train and walk down Astoria. Hang a right onto Steinway Street. A pair of twenty-something women wearing jeans with their hijabs passes me on the sidewalk. Across Steinway is a hookah lounge, a travel agency specializing in pilgrimages to Mecca, and a clothing shop window filled with colorful abayas. I walk past a mosque, several Middle Eastern restaurants, and a halal grocer. Next to the front door a man sits on a kitchen chair smoking a cigarette. He reminds me of Masoud. The whole neighborhood reminds me of Cairo.

I stop when the address on the building matches the back of the postcard. The building is a little shabby—not unlike the *koshary* shop in Giza—but the door frame is tiled in a variety of Egyptian patterns like patchwork and a bronze hand-of-Fatima knocker on the front door makes it feel as if this is the entryway to someone's home instead of a restaurant. I read the address again, even though I know this is the right place, and touch my fingertips to the knocker for good luck. Then I step inside.

The interior is warm and inviting, the air fragrant with the scent of spice and meat. The walls are painted saffron yellow and hung with Egyptian tapestries, gilded mirrors, and artwork with no specific theme. Running along the entire length of one wall is a banquette thrown with dozens of patterned cushions, and hanging over each table is a lantern like the ones I bought at al-Gomaa. It is a restaurant for leisurely meals and long conversation.

"Sit wherever you like and I'll be with you in a moment," a male voice says, and my attention turns sharply away from the lanterns to the kitchen area, which is part of the dining room in the same way the takeaway counter was part of the *koshary* shop. Behind the tiled counter—his back to me as he works a large skillet over a gas flame—is Adam Elhadad.

I don't need to see his face to recognize him. I know the shape of the shoulders that once held my arms up around them. I know that dark curl tucked behind the ear that heard the quiet declarations of my heart. My pulse picks up speed and I stand frozen in the middle of the room, waiting for him to turn around.

And then he does.

He reaches for a menu from a stack at the end of the counter, and when he finally looks up, he stares at me for a long moment, as if I might be a hallucination or a ghost. "Caroline?"

Tears well up in my eyes as I nod. "It's me."

"You're here." The note of wonder in his voice makes me laugh.

I hold up the postcard. "You invited me."

It takes less than a single heartbeat for him to drop the menu on the counter and close the space between us. His body is warm, and the scent of onions and cumin clings to his hair, as his arms crush me against him. I am crying and happy and my world feels *right* again.

"I have imagined this moment so many times," he says, his voice low beside my ear. "But I was afraid you wouldn't come."

"Your postcard showed up in my mailbox yesterday. I came as soon as I could. Why didn't you tell me you were in New York?"

"I wanted to surprise you."

"Mission accomplished," I say. "How long have you been here?"

"I arrived last month but thought I should first get to know Hammad and his family."

"So, wait . . . if you've been here, who sent this postcard?"

"I didn't want to ruin the surprise with a US postage

stamp," Adam says. "So I had Magdi send the card three weeks after my arrival and then hoped you would come."

"If I had known *you* were the gift, I would have been here yesterday."

"It's good you didn't come yesterday. We were very busy."

"I have missed you *so* much."

He touches my face, touches my hair. "It's been the same for me."

"Do your parents know?"

"Yes." He nods. "We talked a long time about you—about the possibility of you—and they realize now that how I feel is serious. They want me to be happy."

I blink back tears and my throat feels too clogged to speak. Adam grins and releases me.

"So. You have arrived at just the right time," he says. "Hammad lets me run the kitchen between lunch and dinner, so you have the restaurant almost entirely to yourself and the best chef of the day."

I laugh. "You should be more confident."

"Come sit." He pulls out a stool at the kitchen counter. "Let me cook for you."

He goes around to the stove and clanks a heavy iron skillet onto the gas burner. My face is flushed with happiness while I watch him sear cubes of lamb and listen as he tells me that after my family left Cairo, he enrolled in culinary school. "I saved all the money from your father," he says. "He always paid me too much."

I think back to that day in Cairo when Mom scolded Dad for being too liberal with the contents of his wallet. "I'm glad."

"For a year I went to school in the morning and waited tables in the evening, but when a kitchen assistant position became available at the hotel, I talked my way into it."

Adam brings me a dish of hummus and a plate of warm, fresh Egyptian bread.

"After I finished school, my father suggested I come to work for my mother's cousin Hammad," he says. "He's a local celebrity because a television show once filmed an episode here. So I'm the waiter when Hammad cooks, but in the afternoons I am allowed the run of the kitchen to practice."

"Best chef of the day."

"Hammad is very skilled," Adam says. "But he basks in the attention and enjoys showing off in the kitchen. Many customers don't mind waiting as he mixes politics and cooking, but others just want to eat."

"How very tactful of you," I say.

He throws a grin over his shoulder as the pan sizzles and the scent of onions and garlic wafts toward me. "Yes, because I'd like to keep my job."

He explains that he lives in an apartment above the restaurant with Hammad's family and shares a room with his two young cousins. "He pays me a fair wage," Adam says. "Not so much that I could afford to live on my own, but enough that my father has been able to pay down the hospital bills and I can keep a small amount for myself. Someday that will change. One day I'll work in a fine kitchen in Manhattan."

"You absolutely will."

A young white couple comes into the restaurant and Adam excuses himself to deliver a pair of menus to the new customers. As he takes their drink order, I scoop hummus onto a bit of bread, then watch as he finishes adding the ingredients to whatever dish he is preparing for me. He still looks like the boy I met in Cairo, but I can see the difference between that Adam and this Adam. This one is making his dreams come true.

"Do you like it here?" I ask as he adds the lamb mixture to a cone-shaped tagine and places it on a metal diffuser to keep the gas flame from cracking the clay pot.

"I have visited some of the museums," he says. "My favorite is the natural history museum, but the city overwhelms me. It is exactly like Cairo and nothing like it at the same time."

"I can imagine how that feels."

He shoots me a knowing grin. "Steinway Street makes me feel like I am at home. In this neighborhood I can speak my own language without people looking at me as if I might be a terrorist, but it's not the same as being with my family."

I can't imagine how *that* feels. In Egypt I never had to fear someone mistaking me for a terrorist. This boy doesn't want to destroy the world; he wants to feed it. Anger washes through me, and I wish I could protect him from the people who refuse to see beyond his skin, who will never know the goodness of his heart.

Adam delivers the drinks and takes the couple's food order, then returns.

"I spend a lot of time here at the restaurant, and on Sundays I go to the Irish pub down the street where they show English football matches," he says. "Liverpool's unpredictability is always consistent. Which is comforting."

Inside the circle of his arms, I thought we could pick up where we left off, that it could be effortless if we let it. But life might be too complicated for love to conquer all. Someday he will go home and we'll go around the same circle again.

"What are you thinking?" Adam asks.

"This is never going to be easy, is it?"

He looks at me with those clear brown eyes, and I see a quick flash of sorrow as he realizes I am right. But then he does the little shrug-nod that makes my chest feel like a cage for my too-big heart. "Perhaps not, but when it comes to you, I would rather have good than easy."

He turns to the stove to begin cooking the new order. And as I watch him, I know we are both right. I have to stop worrying about what might go wrong and just love him back. I take a deep breath and then, finally, loud enough so that Adam Elhadad can hear me, I say just one word.

"*Bahebak.*"

He turns around and gives me that huge smile—the one I can't image ever getting tired of seeing—and we begin again.

ACKNOWLEDGMENTS

In a Perfect World was not meant to be my next book, but sometimes the world has other, better ideas. I owe a debt of gratitude to Sara Sargent, who gave me a seed and a watering can.

Working with Jennifer Ung has been a dream. She understood my vision and helped make it a reality. Big thanks to her and the team at Simon Pulse, including Mara Anastas, Liesa Abrams, Mary Marotta, Lucille Rettino, Carolyn Swerdloff, Catherine Hayden, Michelle Leo, Jodie Hockensmith, Christina Pecorale, Katherine Devendorf, Karina Granda, and Greg Stadnyk.

Kate Schafer Testerman is always in my corner, and I am grateful for everything she does.

Suzanne Young and Cristin Bishara constantly challenge me to be a better writer. I am so fortunate to have them as writing partners and friends.

While researching this book, I had an amazing group of people who answered my questions about Egypt, Islam, and living in Cairo, including Hend El-Nagy, Baasma Aal, Aneeqah N., Aya Elgadaa, Jon Baschshi, Miranda Kenneally, Amanda Ross, and Becky Harrison. Special thanks to Baasma and Aneeqah for reading the earlier drafts, and to Aya for lending her name. If I got anything wrong, it's all on me.

My family is unwavering in their support and patience. Mom, Jack, Caroline, Scott, and Raquella, I love you all . . .

. . . and especially you, Phil.

ABOUT THE AUTHOR

Trish Doller is the author of *Something Like Normal*, which was an ABC New Voices pick and a finalist for NPR's 100 Best-Ever Teen Novels, among many other accolades; *Where the Stars Still Shine*, which was an Indie Next List pick; and *The Devil You Know*. She has been a newspaper reporter, radio personality, and bookseller, and she lives in Fort Myers, Florida, with a relentlessly optimistic Border collie and a pirate.